Frady Bear

Frady Bear

Volume I

by

Brent Tiano

Frady Bear

Published 2025 by 7 Story Rabbit in Highland Beach, Florida, USA. **First Edition.** (Goldenrod)

ISBN: 979-8-9941925-0-4
Library of Congress Control Number: 2026900692

For contact information and merchandise, please visit
www.fradybear.com

In loving memory of those
lost along the way.

While, this fable is loaded with toys, balloons,
fairies, & bears; it contains mature subject matter.
Frady Bear is *not* a children's story.

I sacrificed my *Innocence* to write...
...my *Dignity*, well, that is a different story.
                                    -- Brent Tiano

Acknowledgement

It is impossible to get every word *write* in a book or thank everyone that helped you across the journey. It is incorrect, not to try.

Thank you to my family and friends who encouraged me to try new things, including this book. Janette for loving me, especially when I am tough to love and letting me read aloud my early drafts. Phillip Butera, Celeste Bradley, John Urbancik and Lauren Austin for encouraging me to look, read again, write again and finish.

There are so many people who inspire me. Friends that survived against the odds, people who worked hard and ethically when the world around us ceased to do so. My family, friends and Disney family, who brought music, love, creativity and fun to life. Each of you inspired me to want to do this. Others that reminded me: failure is just a misstep that I will make in the learning something new. And not risking to fail, is the only crime to be ashamed of.

Thank *you*, for taking the time to read this story even in all of its imperfections. I look forward to writing Volume II and hearing your thoughts.

In "Reality"
"Imagination" became
Our only weapon

Prolog

You *think* you already know *me*. You have
read the original stories of Pooh, my friends,
and playing in the hundred acre woods. Piglet
frets he will never be brave, Rabbit fusses to
cure disorganization and Eeyore sulks even as
his friends look for his lost tail. It is true that
these things happened.

We lived a glorious life of innocence,
surrounded by friends with simple troubles,
seeking childhood solutions.

Then one day, Christopher Robin hung a
note on the door to his home tree:
"GONE OUT, BAK SOON."

My cohorts and I continued to fret, fuss and sulk; fully expecting that our boy would return soon to rejoin us. And each day that passed, was much the same as the last. Only minor nuances challenged the unchanging woods which we awoke safely inside each day. Our secluded realm sustained the world we knew and thrived within, providing everything we had and needed.

Why would we suspect that we were a small part of a larger world. *Much* larger.

The life of Pooh, while wonderful, did not prepare me for any world beyond our woods.

The *Imaginary Frontier* is the vast realm containing all the worlds of all the writers in my time. It is built upon the foundation of the words written before and expands with each stroke of a pen or clack of the typewriter. Our Eden was a tiny patch on a vast quilt of overlapping fabrications.

I never dreamt that I would leave the woods, nor what could happen if I did.

If you take a goldfish, won at the county fair, and toss it into a lake, it will grow just to survive. Upon escaping the woods, it was impossible for me not to change into the bear that I am now.

There is a cost, to turning the page. The fish bowl you leave behind, which was once a kingdom, will be outgrown. Innocence lost will never be found.

You may have heard the stories of Pooh, but you don't know what adventures you will share with Frady. Our journey only begins if you turn the page, but the world changes, if you do. It is time for *you* to choose.

Shall we get started?

Once a pawn of time
A toy confronted the storm
Thus a war began

Chapter 1

Tuesday began as each day prior. A yawn, a stretch, and then a rumble in my tummy sends me to forage in the woods for my food.

At first blush, this was to be another ordinary day. The sun would rise soon, which is just how these typical days began.

I had no concept that even an ordinary day could spiral into adventure or that a tiny mistake could lead us into war. I simply knew that my empty belly was calling me to find that sticky something that only bees make.

The woods were quiet;
my friends were still asleep.
I had barely rubbed the sand
from my eyes and hunger had
set my paws into motion.
I was not fully functional
as I walked through the
forest where sweet delirium
resides in a tree guarded
by mere bees.

I'll share with you a secret:

I am not
a storm
cloud.

And yet today,
two storm clouds
met in the sky.

Contrary to popular belief, my life began as a simple toy bear living with friends in the woods. It was a life of fun and joy.

Now a daze, I began each morning out of a need. Just Monday and each day prior, I tightly tied a balloon to my wrist so that I could float gently up to the bee tree opening and fill a jar with honey whilst humming a rain cloud like tune.

On this day, I overslept, and the sun was starting to rise. I had noticed that the bees seem to be extra suspicious once the sun is up; they have been reluctant to share their golden joy in the daylight.

Here, you see, is my critical error. In my rush, I released the balloon *before* I had a grip on the honey jar. This tiny slip was an error of grave consequence. As you have guessed, I need the weight of the jar to slow my ascent. And without it, the balloon carried me straight past the bees, beyond my breakfast, and into the open sky with an empty stomach.

There I dangled, just a small bear, tethered to a balloon, rising faster than I could react. I wanted to scratch my head in wonder, but *that* paw was attached to a runaway balloon. I had no desire to climb further into the sky for a simple head scratch.

I rose even faster than the sun, who peeked over the horizon to view where I was headed. I could clearly see the woods below but none of my friends were awake, yet. As I rose higher, I could see farms, fields of flowers, and even a castle. Previously, I had only flown as high as the treetop – never beyond. I stitched a smile on my face and wondered, where is this balloon taking me?

It was clear skies to the south, east and west. The northern sky, however, was rumbling with foreboding dark shadows.

It is easy to overlook the natural peace that is created in balloon travel. While riding the wind, there is movement across the ground below, and a joining with the air in the sky.

The fur on my neck stood up as a cross wind announced the arrival of the northern storm. An enormous cumulous cloud puffed cold air and then belted out its greeting.

"Whooooooo gooooooooos there?" boomed the cumulus voice.

I was a small and powerless toy bear dangling from a string high above the ground. I drew in a deep breath, and meeker than had hoped to sound, I replied, "I (gulp) might be a storm cloud?"

The true storm flashed an electric smile, shifted its shape, and then thundered

uproariously, "**Buwahahahahaha!**"

Wind whipped past me, and my fur tingled; I wished for an anywhere to hide.

"**You are a brave toy bear, pretending to be a storm in my sky!**" the cloud whispered its smallest thundering voice. "**Go to the west and become this storm you claim to be!**"

Lightning cracked its decree, singeing the fur on my arm, as thunder roared through me. A mighty gust whipped us into the western skies.

For hours, I flew over hills, forestlands, and valleys. I drifted past a jeweled city, a tall castle, a dark bog, and a shimmering sea. I lazily chased the sun from one horizon to the other. After dusk, even the balloon grew tired of me, and we slipped downward toward the treetops.

The wind briskly escorted us across a wide river, then over a village nestled along its edge.

Wafting smoke from chimneys delivered scents of dinner and comfort. Laughter rose up, to be followed by shouts of greeting. Creatures ran below, trying to keep pace with us as the breeze whisked us overhead. Some creatures even waved, and I waved back!

I was excited to see faces, even the faces of strangers. I felt like a celebrity! I was so distracted with the commotion below that I didn't notice the approach of the giant wall.

OOPH!

I slammed into this giant, immovable slab of stone! Stars exploded behind my eyes, and my body went limp. The balloon released my paw from its grip and slipped away into the night. I was left clinging to the wall, high above the ground.

The curtain of darkness had dropped during sunset. I could neither see the ground below nor how high the wall rose above me.

One at a time, searchlights popped on and glared upon me from the distance. The shouts below were less friendly, now. A siren wailed in the distance, and a new commotion grew on the ground below.

My paws grew moist, panic filled my fibers, and gravity tugged downward on me.

"Let go" a gentle whisper rose through the noise, saying again, "Trust me and let go."

So, I did.

✦

Pooh remnants cling to
Fictional dividing wall
Flush with memories

Chapter 2

Wednesday began as each day prior, except I wasn't in my own bed. Also, my head was bandaged, my arm had a storm cloud burned onto it, and a panda with an eye patch was staring at me.

The bear smiled, rose onto his hind legs, and spoke in a deep, calm voice. "I am Spook, you are in my home, and you are safe, for now. When you feel up for it, come get some tea."

Still groggy, I climbed out of bed and wobbled toward the kitchen. Passing by a collection of sewing tools, I wondered if other bears craved HONEY the way I do.

I climbed up the larger than myself chair, as Spook poured a steaming cup of tea. I sniffed the cup, then sipped on the ginger tea until the heat overwhelmed my lips.

"Who are you?" asked Spook as he tilted the kettle to fill his own teacup.

I rubbed the bump on my head, which throbbed again, and reminded me of the stonewall encounter yesterday.

The question should have been easy to answer. I am sure that I had a name and used it frequently, before I smacked the wall of forgetting. At this tender moment, my sore brain failed to locate the answer to this simple question. So, in all honesty, I replied, "Fraid I can't recall who I'm meant to be right now."

The panda's brow scrunched up, and there was a long pause as he thought.

"Let's condense that thought to 'Frady.' Frady the bear. What *do* you remember, if anything?" he inquired.

I stitched a smile onto my face, as I liked the way 'Frady' sounded.

"Have you any honey?" I asked, hopefully scanning the room for a HONEY-looking jar.

The panda shook his head, "no" and smiled. I saw nothing to fix this specific hunger in the kitchen. But after a full day with nothing to drink, even ginger tea was sweet mercy to an empty belly. To answer his question, I jogged my memories to see what I could recall.

"It was a Tuesday, though it's mostly the same every day, not just on Tuesdays. Once again, I bound my paw tight with string. My eyes gleamed with anticipation of the sweet taste. My mind reeled with the feeling I get when honey drips from my paw to my mouth. My stomach made anticipatory grumbles to join in the chorus of angels that sang the praise of HONEY!

Deep in the bee tree, the stingers guard their sweet, sticky treasure. I crave it all day, dream it at night, and lick it off my paws until the fur loses all sweetness.

Above me is a noisy beehive. Beside me a sad, empty jar. Tethered to my wrist is a large, red balloon that I had inflated for the launch.

Operation Storm Cloud began as a non-destructive invasion attempting to borrow enough honey to savor, fulfill, and satisfy me…"

Spook raised his uncovered eyebrow, "You *borrow* honey?"

"Well, I borrowed the *honey jar*, that I return with each morning, and they don't seem to mind."

Spook shrugged and I continued.

"Yesterday, I launched the balloon before grabbing the *borrowed* honey jar. Without the jar as my ballast, I shot into the sky where I encountered a storm cloud. This cloud was *not impressed* with my impersonation of a storm. He branded my arm and sent me here on a gust of wind."

I stopped for another sip of tea with one paw while showing off my new storm cloud branded on the other paw.

"The storm winds carried me west, over flowered fields, crystal towers, broken castles, dense woods and a glimmering sea.

My hopes for a soft landing were shattered as I literally struck the tallest wall I had never seen before. When I woke up, I was here."

"I assume that you don't have your passport or origin story, since this adventure was accidental?" he asked.

"What?"

"You've crossed story lines without editorial approvals, proper authorship, or even copyrights. Even though it was an accident, your arrival in the town of Fringe is completely illegal. And when…" Spook stopped talking and glanced at the ceiling. Then, pressing a finger to his lips. *"Shhhhh!"*

My teacup rattled on the saucer. The table shook, and my chair rattled. Ripples formed on the surface of the tea. Outside, but somewhere near, thousands of feet marched in cadence, stirring the leaves in my teacup.

Spook sprang into action. He reached for the saltshaker and peeled a small dot from its metal cap. He turned from the table, then affixed the hole to the wall, and looked me in the eyes.

"I have to hide you," he whispered. "So be still and keep quiet. Do you understand?"

I nodded.

He touched the hole with two fingers, which dilated, and then I crawled inside. He squeezed the edges, and the hole closed effortlessly around me until only a pinhole in the wall remained. He dumped out my cup and slipped it into the sink.

Enveloped in darkness, I put my eye to the tiny hole, watching and listening intently to learn what I could learn.

The marching came to an abrupt stop and was followed by a pounding on a door nearby. Pressed against the mortar, inside the wall, I could hear lock unbolt and a door hinge creak.

"I know he is here!" barked a militant voice. "We have a warrant to search your premises."

Cool as snow, Spook responded, "Search if you must, but I don't have the first clue of what you seek to find."

From inside the makeshift safe room, hundreds of marching boots drummed over the rest of their conversation. A platoon of armored centipedes, each one about half my length, tromped uniformly back and forth across the floor. The thumps of hundreds of feet hammered the floor, walls and ceilings as they literally crawled over every inch. Dust sifted down on my head as they tromped over my location.

At last, the officer at the front door screamed, "This was a waste of time!" And the marching returned to the street. The door clicked shut, and locks slid back into place.

Eventually, Spook returned to remove me from the bunker. The hole blossomed again, and Spook hauled me out. Spook peeled up the hole and placed it back on the saltshaker.

"You must leave the Fringe. You can't stay in this town any longer," he said. "They will search again, and you can't be here when they come back."

I didn't understand until he handed me a poster with a picture of a bear and a balloon. It had more than one language on it. What I could read, read: 'Wanted,' 'Reward,' and 'NICE.'

"What do the 'NICE' people want with me?" I asked.

"They are neither 'nice' nor 'people.' They are agents of NICE: **N**on-**I**maginary, **C**ontainment, and **E**xpulsion," he explained.

"You are a Non-Imaginary who arrived in the town of Fringe illegally," said the black and white bear. "And *when* they capture you, they *will* deport you, or *worse*."

I was certain that my future was unraveling at the seams. "But the *storm* blew me here!" I protested.

Spook was on the move, again. He thrust an ill-fitting, overcoat onto me and jammed a felt fedora over my fuzzy ears.

"Keep the brim low. This is your disguise for now," he said. "You need to look like you belong here."

The hat was old and tilted over one ear. The tired overcoat was sooty, had a hole in the pocket and frayed edges. It wasn't a great disguise, as I looked like a toy bear in a small hat and an oversized coat.

Spook tossed random things into a backpack and placed me inside before he put the backpack on. We moved to the door.

✦

Frady Bear

Green eyed monster
Remove the claws of justice
Bound in dilemma

Chapter 3

With a quick look around, Spook closed the door to his simple home, and we left.

Spook moved quickly through the streets with me tucked into his backpack. I was a fugitive in the town of Fringe on the western border of the Imaginary Frontier. Peeking out the back, I watched to see if we were being followed.

I now know that the village of Fringe was built with materials discarded in the real world and smuggled into the Imaginary Frontier. While made of waste from the Real, the craftsmanship in the Fringe was excellent.

Proper homes of brick and mortar were joined by smaller homes made of boxes, tin sheeting, and cargo crates. Each wall was conjoined to another, forming shanty condos which lined the cobblestone streets. This area of the Fringe had all sizes of dwellings stuffing each nook and cranny not already dedicated to the street.

It made sense. In a village with bears, raccoons, centipedes, and who knows what other creatures, the homes were customized to fit the various shapes and sizes.

Spook zigzagged through winding streets following the edge of the wall that denied my flight into the real world - the same wall that separated the realm of the Real from Imaginary Frontier.

The streets were quiet at this late hour in the night. Peeking out of the backpack, I spotted mice, dogs, and maybe an opossum? The creatures moved quickly between the shadows to avoid attention.

We turned a corner and passed through a wrought-iron gate into a small garden before an entry door. Spook looked back to verify that we were alone, and I noted that this house was lavish compared to the surrounding homes.

Spook pulled a brass chain, and a deep chime echoed on the other side of the solid door. Spook followed the chime with a coded knock and stepped into the light.

There was a long pause while we waited for something to happen. Perhaps it was too late for a visit? Maybe we weren't welcome? In the distance, a siren wailed, and Spook shifted nervously from one paw to the other.

A possum (definitely a possum) ran past the gate with scraps dangling from its mouth.

A shuffling came from inside, and then a mirrored periscope studied the front stoop.

Ding! Chimed a new bell, and the heavy door unlatched. Spook pushed inside, and we were met by a fancy carpeted floor and a room filled with toys and trinkets. The door swung closed behind us and latched again. The lights were low, but it was brighter than outside. Spook removed the backpack and held it in front of him so that I could see out.

The center of the room was lit with an electric chandelier of sorts. On the far wall was a series of carpeted stairs which led up to a perch with a wide black pillow. A regal Russian Blue cat with emerald eyes silently peered down at Spook.

Neither spoke.

From out of the darkness, a ragged mouse bolted across a beam on the roof and leapt to the ledge in front of the cat. The exhausted mouse struggled for breath. Now that he was stationary, I could see the mouse's tail had been bitten short, ears tattered, and there were patches of missing fur. He lowered his eyes from the cat's gaze.

"Give your report!" said the cat in a low, threatening voice.

The mouse focused its full attention on the cat as it inhaled deeply to respond.

"NICE raided the panda's place," huffed the mouse in a breathy but strong voice for such a tiny creature.

"AND?" growled the cat impatiently.

The mouse lowered its head further, and continued, "They searched and left with nothing. I waited and watched until the panda fled."

"Is that ALL?" demanded the cat.

"That is *all* I could see from the tree, but I didn't see a toy bear."

"Go to the roof and watch for troops." He hissed at the cowering mouse.

The mouse bowed even lower and scampered into the rafters.

"REALLY?!" growled Spook when the coast was clear.

"I monitor you and the others," said the indignant cat. "Nothing is simple since the war began." He paused. "What do you want from me?" he asked as his tail flit to the side.

Spook thought for a moment, then opened the backpack. I climbed out and stood to face the cat.

"You are the only one I trust with…" Spook began.

"Trust!? You can't trust *ANYONE* right now. Not the toy. Not you. Not even me!" interrupted the cat. "Get rid of the jacket."

"You have traveled the Frontier, know the check points and how to avoid them. You have connections," replied Spook as I slipped off the coat.

"NICE came here last night. They asked about the toy, where it came from, what it meant, and where to find it." The cat shifted uncomfortably. "They asked the questions again, and then they took my claws one at a time. I told them anything to get them to stop. Lies, truth, stories – I told them anything." He slipped out a bandaged, bloody paw that he had been concealing under his body.

The cat looked away with a mix of anger and shame. "I cannot help you, the toy, or anyone. I am just an indoor cat, now."

Spook looked down at me and sighed. "What about him?"

"You saved him, so he is your responsibility, unless you think he can cross the Imaginary Frontier alone?" He waited for a moment, cocked his head, and then continued. "You do realize that my home is being watched, now?"

Spook's shoulders fell, and he lifted me into the backpack before slipping it on.

"Think!" hissed the cat, laying his ears flat. "If you are going to succeed in this journey, then first imagine how you succeed and then live the hero version of this story."

The mouse rushed in with wide eyes. Sable winced slightly as he tucked his paws out of view.

"Let me guess," interrupted Sable, pointing his ears at the front door. The mouse nodded.

Sable spoke calm and hypnotically, "If you want to survive, you will exit out the back door, now." he paused. "Or you can simply hand him over."

"Goodbye." Spook threw on the backpack

and sprinted to the back door.

The back door was reinforced but easily sprung open from within. The alley was dim and lit only by moonlight. Small animals rummaged through the garbage in search of scraps. The creatures eyed us with a mix of fear and curiosity. We approached the main street with caution as we could hear the fast-marching centipedes on the move. Spook turned away from the noise, the imposing wall, and ran east toward the river.

A loud whistle shrieked at us, and Spook dropped on all four paws into a sprint. I bounced wildly inside the backpack until we came to a sudden halt.

I could smell the nearby garbage and hear his heavy breathing. We were hiding in an alley behind a pile of trashcans. Most of the centipedes ran past the alley, but three of the creatures turned into the alley to search for us. As the noisy creatures closed in on our hiding spot, Spook heaved a garbage can at them. It landed with a metallic crash, crushing two of the soldiers. The third centipede darted to the street and let out a high-pitched hiss. The cadence broke stride, and their comrades circled back for us.

Spook dropped to the ground and searched around. Finding a manhole cover, he mightily lifted it from the street. He sniffed and then lowered us into the hole. He pulled the iron lid back into place.

We descended into the tunnel and waited for a moment as our eyes adjusted to the darkness of the sewer. The tunnel was cool, damp, and smelled awful. Spook sniffed the tunnel left and right and then chose a direction. We moved forward for quite a while. Eventually, it grew light as we emerged into open air at the river's edge.

Spook gathered his orientation and then moved quickly downstream along the water's edge. The banks were overgrown with shrubs. Spook wound along the narrow path until he spotted something hidden in a thicket.

Carefully, he pulled away the strategically placed branches to reveal a small canoe. He pushed the small boat into the water, situated himself, and we were quickly away from the shore. I could hear and feel him rowing. Behind us, I could see the wall looming above the town, and the shore receding away from us. Out of breath, Spook dropped the paddle into the boat, took off the backpack, and set me onto the other seat of the boat.

Now facing him, he took a minute to size me up. As he caught his breath, I asked the first of my questions. "Is this your boat?"

"No," he smiled. "It's a bit small for me, but Sable won't be needing it, anymore."

He picked up the paddle and rowed further away from Fringe. He seemed to be deciding what to tell me or where to start.

At last, he spoke again. "We have been perched on the edge of war for a long time, and you cast the deciding vote."

"I just got here!" I said defensively.

The panda sucked in a deep breath as he continued to paddle away from the giant wall and all of its chaos.

"Yes, and your arrival was misread. The great council had been debating how to respond to the attacks coming from the Real side of the wall. There was to be a signal to be given once a decision had been made. And you floated conspicuously across the countryside on a red balloon. The residents of Fringe believe your flight was the signal that the council had chosen to join the war.

I scratched my head as the impassioned bear continued. "Your honey craved misadventure has become the symbolic declaration of war on the Realm of the Real."

"I am just a bear who gets hungry for honey," I said. "It was a mistake."

I looked past the tired panda, beyond the wall, and at the moon in the sky. It smiled a wan smile at me, even as I wondered how a silly toy, pretending to be a storm cloud, had landed miles from home and managed to launch a war.

I had to wonder if I was really prepared for what would happen next, but moving forward was the only way to know.

Between the rhythmic "swoosh" of the oar, the cold of the night, and exhaustion, I surrendered to sleep.

✦

River of denial
Wayward island of remorse
Cauldron boiling black

Chapter 4

Today began as no day should. Childish whoops filled my ears even before my paws had rubbed the sand from my eyes.

Our little canoe had beached on a rocky island, and a small tribe of youths greeted us with shrieks, antics, and spears taller than me. It was an odd group of children. They were too young to be sure if they were boys or girls. They were all dressed in onesies with animal hoods, like you might see at Halloween. And some of them even had tails that dragged in the sand behind them.

The costumed clan was frightening with their tribal antics and lively shouting. A raccoon dressed child reached the canoe before we could push back into the river.

Honestly, I think Spook could have taken the lot of them, if he had been more awake or even mildly aggressive. The feral kids pointed their spears at us and walked us ashore.

As we made our way onto the jungle island, we heard exotic birds, which competed with the laughing kids for who was the loudest. I didn't have to struggle to keep up with this group, as the smallest child was only slightly taller than myself with his rabbit ears up. Spook walked casually on his hind legs, while sniffing at the air ahead.

Emerging from the jungle was a fort crafted out of the largest trees and connected to neighboring trees by vines. Ladders, platforms, swings, and hammocks protruded from branches at dizzying heights. A rope ladder was tossed down to us. Spook put me in the backpack, and the group climbed into the branches. Upon reaching the first landing of many, Spook set me onto the bamboo shoots that were lashed together as flooring.

The fort wasn't much to look at from a civilized standard, but it was all-out amazing for kids living on a jungle island. Bamboo chairs, coconut bowls, and makeshift items were strewn everywhere, as there didn't seem to be a mom to pick up after them.

"Ears-spay own-day!" cried out the tallest yet of the costumed warriors in a fierce tiger suit. The group of children beamed with pride and stepped back to show off their captives. Spook looked a little pensive or possibly annoyed but kept his cool all things considered.

"*Peak-say a-tin-lay?*" asked the unnamed tall one.

"*Es-yay.* I am Spook. And this" he said, referring to me "is Frady, who does not understand your Pig Latin."

"I am Grrrreg" introduced the tiger boy in English with a growl. "Our scouts caught you sneaking onto our island."

"You are a real boy, who lives on an imaginary island. I need to take this toy to council, so we can avoid the war."

"Lies! You are our prisoner," stated Grrreg.

"I am a tired and need food and a bed," grunted Spook.

"*Age-cay em-thay!*" demanded the tall boy.

Promptly, a bamboo cage slipped down from high above. The homemade cage looked solid enough as we were ceremoniously shoved inside. The door was tied closed, and we were raised high above the main level of the tree fort into smaller branches.

Spook circled three times and nestled down to rest his eyes. I tried to ask where we were and what was happening, but he waved me off before slipping into a loud, snoring sleep.

I examined the cage to see if I could slip out, but the bamboo prison was just too tight for my head to slip through. The slats didn't prevent me from watching the antics of the animal tribe below.

On the sands near the tree's massive trunk, I witnessed the hoopla and excitement as a veritable zoo shouted and chanted in their exotic tongue. The caged panda continued to snore and dream bear visions. I know for certain that honey, home, and friends haunt my sleep visions to this day. While watching Spook, I wondered if real panda's dreams were like mine.

The warm day wandered off as dusk arrived, and Spook stretched from his sleep. Far below, torches were lit and shadows danced in campfire light. Spook opened his eye and sniffed the air.

"Are we going to be here a while?" I asked. This was my third day with no honey, and that weighed on my mind.

"I doubt it." he paused, perhaps to add drama. "They will either let us go or..." Again, he stopped. "Or they could make a costume with your hide, cook me for dinner, and then make an over-sized panda onesie."

"I am a toy bear!"

"And you're just the right size for the smallest child" smiled Spook.

"Who will stop them from cooking you?" I asked.

"You are very observant" he shrugged.

Spook stood on all fours, as the cage was

too low for him to stand. He stretched one shoulder and then the other and looked happier having slept a bit.

The tiger and the raccoon boys approached with their spear sticks, below.

We were lowered down, the cage door released. They marched us to the bonfire we had eyed below. The incessant whooping and hollering grew louder with our arrival. A huge kettle boiled on the bonfire as we were led to the center of the celebration.

"And-a-pay! And-a-pay! AND-A-PAY!" they chanted.

The tiger boy pointed at Spook and then the pot. Spook shook his head. Spears dropped into the attack position, and Spook bared his teeth.

The tiger boy lunged at Spook, who snatched the spear and crushed it to splinters in his bamboo shredding jaws. A rabbit boy gripped my arm to drag me out of the fray, and the panda spread his claws to swat.

The shadows ceased to dance, and a tall one darted between Spook and the scared rabbit boy. All went quiet, and Spook held his fighting stance.

From out of the twilight flew a large male sprite, who smiled and winked at Spook. Hands wide open, the sprite announced, "If anyone has abused our guests, they will be sent home!"

Oddly, this was far worse than being boiled alive or swatted by a panda, and a hush rippled through the sleep over party.

"Welcome to Neverland! Join our celebration and tell me your story. I am Pete!" he said with a bow and flew to the head table. "This is the Lobo Tribe."

The rabbit scampered back into the group. Spook dropped on all fours, and we walked over to the long table covered with treats. Behind us, a shadow sprite resumed its dancing.

"Lobos?" I asked.

"Lobo is short for Lost Boys. Children and orphans who are hiding from the Real Realm," Peter explained.

Each child earned its spirit animal and remained the age he arrived at the island until he chose to leave. Peter is the chief of Neverland and recruited new boys to the tribe from the Realm. If one of the boys truly got out of hand, as punishment, he was sent home, never to return.

In many ways, Neverland served as a halfway house between the Realm and the Imaginary Frontier. Some of the boys lived and played on the island even longer than they had existed in the Real world. And for some, this family was more of a family than they had experienced before. He then asked about us.

Spook explained that we had escaped the wall city and were headed toward the council to square things up, as we ate a feast of local fruits, fish, and toasted coconuts. The party roared to life with hooting, drumming, and jumping.

It all ended suddenly when a firework tumbled out of the sky and rolled across the table in front of Peter. A tiny, winged sprite peered up at Peter with wide eyes and then started shouting in her high-pitched voice.

"We are under attack! Neverland is besieged!" she yelled.

Her wings frayed from extreme flight, her fairy dress was torn, and she took a moment to catch her breath. She looked like she had flown without regard through thorn bushes to deliver this message.

The wild boy's party noise died as Peter stood and picked up his tiny friend.

"These are friends," he said, referring to us.

"No! You can't see the invaders. I watched Hook, his crew, and ship unravel into black puddles and wash into the sea."

"Hook is gone?" gasped Peter.

A howl rang out from the Lobos, but Peter waved them off.

"If they can erase Hook, they can destroy me, Tink, or Neverland!"

"What about the boys?" I asked.

"They are from the real!" he thought aloud. "But they *would* drown if the island were to be unwritten!"

"So would we," chimed Spook.

At that moment, the color literally drained from her body, and her limbs ran together.

"No!" screamed Pete as her tiny figure melted. Ink pooled under her feet, and she collapsed onto the bamboo table before draining her life onto the sand below.

In shock, Peter paled as Spook picked me up with one hand and tossed me into the backpack. The previous color never really returned to Peter's face.

"We must get to our canoe!" Spook shouted at Peter.

The pale boy pointed into the darkness, and his shadow led the way. I peered back as the Lobos raced after us toward the beach. Peter air lifted the slowest creature and flew ahead to the fleet of canoes. The island rumbled beneath us. Trees shed leaves which became ink drops that rained down on us. Color dulled and drained in all directions, leaving mere line drawings of an island jungle.

Spook dropped to all fours and bolted to the beach. Peter deposited the rabbit child in a tribal canoe and circled back for the next straggling lost boy.

The costumed paws splashed and blackened as the island's sand coalesced into a slurry of ink. The tree fortress collapsed behind us as we neared the shore. Screaming children fled in terror as their imaginary world melted.

Grrrreg ran back to aid the fallen raccoon as we reached the shore. Spook jumped into our little boat and pushed us away from the gurgling chaos. Upon arrival at the shore, the Lobos jumped into canoes and took up paddles. The last stragglers splashed through the deepening black mud near the water's edge.

Peter dropped the second small boy who was caught by Grrreg in a canoe. The sprite fell into the deepening black muck. He arched his back and shouted to the frightened tribe.

"You must go home, back to your homes in the Real!" he rasped. "I cannot take you there. Stay together! Find your way, home."

His arms buckled and his head splashed into the syrup. His fist rose up and for a moment I had hope. His head breached the tar and gasped for air. "Remember Neverland!" he gurgled, "Remember me..." and slipped beneath the surface of a growing black pool.

Even his hat dissolved as the living stared on. The island dissolved into a film on the water as the tribe gathered their small fleet. Peter's shadow flickered, then fell (without a splash) to vanish into moonlit reflections.

I climbed out of the pack and Spook placed me onto the crossbeam. I stared across the vast waters darkened with ink that once created an island. I wondered if this same fate was coming for me, for Spook, for all of us?

Spook turned the canoe to face the homeless boys. The older lads were red in the face and sour. The young ones were shocked into silence while the smallest rabbit sobbed.

"You need to row west, toward the wall. There is a gate in the wall in the middle of Fringe. Stay together, if you can and get through the gate," Spook spoke. He was loud, firm and portrayed an adult level of calm.

"Can you take us there?" asked the tiger

boy.

"No, we are headed south to the Dreamlands" he paused. "Work as a tribe, row toward the lights in the west, and you will be fine. Start now, and you will be there in the morning. Tell them what you witnessed!"

The boys dipped their paddles and a small voice called out "Stroke!" at regular intervals. They slowly pulled away, against the current to the west.

I eyed Spook, who watched them to see that they progressed. A single tear welled up before passing down his furry cheek. He lifted the paddle, directing the small boat away from the *truly* lost boys toward the rising moon.

"What will happen to them?" I asked.

"They don't belong here," he paused. "I don't know, what will happen, but we can't go back to the Fringe, and they have to get out of the IF."

"This looks more like a east than south?"

"We are headed east," he confirmed.

Frady Bear

"Not to the Dreamlands?"

"No, never there."

Unwritten story
And the promise of never
Be forgotten woes

Chapter 5

I stood on the bow and looked to the east. The moon had risen and smiled as it shone the way. Spook pulled us closer to tomorrow with each stroke and further from the past destruction. Even in the dark, I could see the ink stains from our close call on the oar's blade.

The adrenaline high from our flight intoxicated my thoughts with what could have happened. Eventually, the cool night air sobered my focus back to the current situation.

I turned to face the panda and sat on the bow. My mind filled with questions, but my mouth seemed stuffed with more than the usual cotton fibers.

"Mmmm Hmmm." I cleared my throat to gain permission to speak. Spook continued to look past me at the waters that lay ahead.

"What happened to the island?" I asked. I counted the strokes of the oar and was well into double digits before he responded.

"There are reports of kingdoms in the Imaginary Frontier which had been unwritten to one degree or another. Castles crumbling, individuals melting or deformed into a sliver of their being." He paused. "But I had never seen it. I would never imagine the demise of an entire kingdom. That was an absolute mythocaust. The complete loss of a story."

I could sense the change of heart as the shock of events wore off, and the sadness of the finality crept in.

"That couldn't happen to us, could it?" I asked.

"To you," he whispered. "I cannot be unwritten in this or any realm. Even though I live here in the Imaginary Frontier; I am from the Realm of the Real and, like the Lost Boys, cannot be unwritten as such."

"Am I not real?" I blinked.

"Yes, here you *are* real."

"And yet, I can be unwritten?"

"You, your home, your friends, the bee tree, your story…" he grunted as he pulled into the water, "it can all be erased in this war."

"Why?"

He shrugged.

In my adventures, I had temporarily forgotten about home. I had been so busy surviving the *now*, that I had forgotten about *then*. And then, my mind returned to me, as it frequently does. I wondered who would miss *me* if I were unwritten along with my home and friends. Without them, (or myself), would anyone even know to miss me? This seemed too important a question to ponder alone.

"Spook? Will you make an effort to remember me, if I am ever unwritten?" I asked at last.

He turned his eyes from the horizon and stopped rowing to stare at me.

"You are the toy bear who physically left a mark on the great wall. You are Frady the Bear who managed to escape the NICE People in the village of Fringe. And you are the witness to the erasing of Neverland."

"But if all of my friends and I become spots of ink, who will remember?"

He looked me in the eye and said, "You are now a friend of mine, and therefore, will never be forgotten."

I felt relieved.

"Let's stop this war from happening at all." I said as he returned to paddling the canoe.

✦

Rose covered grasses
Gardens of sheared delight
Tulips of gossip

Chapter 6

The sunrise over the sea was as welcome as ever a sunrise could be. Neither of us had really slept, and I had given up on any ordinary type of day for the near future.

In the distance a forest of tiny trees appeared, and with every oar stroke the trees grew slightly larger. Long before the appearance of the shore, an eerie wailing drifted across the water. As the beach came into view, I spotted what I suspected was making this dreadful sound.

The noisy creature appeared to have the head, legs, and tail of a cow protruding from a giant turtle shell. Within reach of the turtle-cow was a huge pile of long-stemmed roses.

I had never heard a cow cry before. Yet

here she was eating rose petals, arranging the stems, and wailing between bites.

Spook paddled us up to the beach and stepped out of the canoe to pull us ashore. I jumped down from the bow and cautiously approached the mournful creature, since she was much larger than myself. Her tears streamed onto the beach, pooled in the sand, and trailed on into the sea.

She finished chewing the rose off a stem and arranged it neatly beside the previously chewed stem. Only as I drew near did I realize that the deflowered stems now served as memorial tick marks which continued down the beach as far as I could see.

"Halloo, what causes your suffering?" I asked from a safe distance.

The cow-thing turned her head and gave me a look that only a cow-thing can muster. She turned her back, moaned louder and consumed another rose. She was content to ignore me and continued thus until the real bear came into her view. Her brown eyes widened with disbelief.

"Spook? Is that you?" asked the creature in disbelief between bites.

The panda replied, "Yes, Verni, it's me."

The rose devouring ritual stopped for a moment as she whispered, "Look what they've done to Wo..." she sputtered, "Wonder..." She sighed and inhaled deeply "the garden" she finished teasing a rose into her mouth.

"Wonderland?" he finished. She nodded.

I looked past the beach, and there was much to witness. What once was an amazing garden, filled with animals, plants, statues, and topiaries, now displayed carnage. Statues toppled, cages emptied, and a distant iron gate was thrown open. The rose bushes that had once surrounded the garden perimeter were uprooted and strung upside down from the ornate fence. Every single one of the rose bushes had been literally de-flowered.

From within her shell, she produced a handkerchief, and Verni wiped her nose. Tinged with hurt, she spoke again, "If you've come to save us - you are too late."

The black and white bear sighed and sat on the beach beside her. He took off his backpack and reached much further than his hand should go in such a small bag. After a moment of fumbling, he produced an ornate, wooden box. He presented it to the sad creature, which mooed and pushed it away between bites.

Spook set it down within reach and opened the lid. Clear metallic notes pinged out a tiny concert of music. Her chewing synced up with the rhythm. For a moment, her crying ceased, and she just listened to the melody before it came to rest.

"We seek the Hatter," Spook said. "Is he still here?"

"He is" she sighed, "and he is dangerous."

"You mean mad?" he smiled.

"Not at all what I meant," she stated. "Be careful. This 'war' has changed him. We do what we have to, now."

He closed the box and re-opened it. The mechanical melody began again.

"We inspire music, *their* music and they fight to destroy us?" she pondered aloud. "How does it make any sense?" She placed another stem on the beach as she chewed before taking another rose from the pile.

"Keep this" he responded. "You need a little happiness, and it lightens my load."

Spook stood up, brushed off the sand and slipped on the backpack. I felt a little put off, never having been addressed or introduced, but I told myself to just let it go.

As we walked to the garden, the music box continued, and the weeping created harmony between the bites.

We stepped over the rose stem arrangements in the sand onto the stairs that married the beach to this garden. A wrought-iron fence, adorned with thorn bushes, defined the garden's edge. The garden was acres across and still home to a variety of plant life. The overgrown sunflowers slowly turned their gaze away from us. Snapdragons withheld their gossiping to silently stare as we passed. Even the bed of mushrooms lowered their caps to avoid eye contact. The violets whispered loudly to each other about our intrusion on their gated beds.

Unable to contain my disappointment, I asked Spook, "Why didn't you introduce me?"

"Not here, not now" he answered.

Clearly, this was not the friendly forest of *my* home. I was thrilled to exit the gate leaving the hostile garden behind. Outside the front gate, stood an enormous tree with branches reaching in every direction and roots that extended well beyond our feet. After the cultivated dejection we experienced in the garden, I wondered if this tree also bore unfriendly fruit.

Then from the gnarliest of branches, deep in its shadow, it smiled at me.

"Halloooo!" I waved and smiled back.

Spook looked at me sharply, and I wondered if I had erred in being friendly. It was then; everything became a little strange.

✦

Chess verses checkers
Questioned tree of knowledge
Teeth riddled smile

Chapter 7

A fuzzy checkered tail, flit back and forth amongst the branches. Slowly, a black and white checkered cat appeared to claim the smile and the tail perched in the tree.

"Halloooo! How are you?" I asked even as Spook silently shook his head at me.

"I am half here, half there, and *always* grinning at the outcome. You are?" he parried, with a hypnotic purr of a voice.

"Cheshire Cat?" Spook greeted and bowed.

"Just Chess," he corrected with a sharp smile. "The 'shire' has gone with the dodo bird and taken the 'Wonder' from the land with it. Only those willing to exchange their spots for stripes are here, today."

"Chess, I am Frady, Frady Bear." I jumped in so as not to be left out of this conversation, too.

"Ah, new stripes for you as well," he grinned neither pleasantly nor unpleasantly. I pondered his comment.

Spook seemed to understand the need for specificity when conversing with Chess. "Who still remains in Wonderland?" he asked.

"Many remains are *in* Wonderland, and those *alive* are born again," he riddled. His body flickered with an unwavering grin.

"The Hatter?"

"The kettle boils hot, but the steep has turned bitter. Madness is the main course when the host has one body but occupies every seat."

"Let us find some tea," Spook said to me. "Until we meet, again Chess!"

I turned to say goodbye, but most of the checkered cat had already vanished.

✦

Friends, spies, patriots
Miss fortune favors the brave
Party 'til past dark

Chapter 8

We trotted away from the giant smiling tree
and through the ruins of what had once been
Wonderland. As if an angry dragon had
rampaged through the town, some homes were
reduced to limestone rubble, others burned out
shells, and others remained unscathed. The
realm would have been church-quiet except for
the whispering tulips that peeked out as we
walked past.

I found it a mystery that Neverland could
be completely unwritten while Wonderland
was still intact.

Ahead loomed a wooden house that wore
a wiled look of physical insanity. Its shutters
were boarded tightly over windows, while
completely absent from others. It was both
painted in splotches of festive colors, and

naked wood in other areas. The iron gate was locked tight, while the wooden fence had posts removed for easy entry to the yard. Jovial music was playing from the far side of the house.

Spook rapped twice on the gate, before slipping through the fence. My cotton fibers shrank with warning, but my hunger and curiosity coaxed me into the yard. I slipped through the fence into the event trodden lawn. Wisteria clung to the front trellis and whistled with alarm as we approached the house.

The festive mess trailed around the home, so we followed the porch around the building to seek its owner. Looking at the aged streamers, trampled confetti and flowers growing through broken cups, a party of elimination was nearing its end.

The heavy wooden table sat on the lawn, surrounded by a dozen or more mismatched chairs. Cups and saucers were stacked into towers of precarious heights, a handful of teapots were staggered across the table, and a smattering of pastries lingered on platters for willing participants to imbibe.

Our host was swaying to the music on a chair at the head of the table, stacking an even larger fine porcelain tower. He looked like a cross between a circus clown and a ringmaster in his multi-colored suit and silk top hat. He had wild hair and a crooked bowtie with polka dots. He seemed quite alone at the event as he focused his attention on this delicate endeavor.

Spook cautiously approached the table with, "Hello? Is it teatime?"

"There is[th] always[th] time for tea, no matter how late you are." the man said in a sing-song voice and a slight lisp, never shifting his eyes from the tipsy tower.

"Is this seat available?" I asked, surveying the table for edible bites as I climbed onto an upholstered armchair.

"Libertea is[th] the "tea" I protect, in this oppressed realm," he replied and nodded at me with a slight curtsey as he stretched for another saucer.

I grabbed for a cookie and hungrily devoured it. The wafer was both stale and delicious in the way that hunger for everything creates appreciation of anything.

"Wonderland is rumored to be the sanest realm of all, these days," fished Spook as he settled in the seat between myself and our host.

"Ha!" retorted man in an overblown manner. His exaggerated reaction caused the tower to fall. He jumped off the chair and seized the spotted teapot. Stopping at every seat, he poured tea into the cups enroute to ours. Spook received a full cup of tea, but the pot ran dry before he got me.

"Be a dear and pass Mr. Cuddles a full spot of tea, would you?" he asked Spook, and danced back to the head of the table.

Spook handed me a cup from his right, as the absent owner surely would not miss it.

He continued with a lisp, "Perhapsth our sanity skipped out, when the plague of war marched in. It was a witch's haunt and den of spies." He pranced to his seat and waved his tiny cup. "Cheers!"

"A witch's *haunt?*" Spook primed the conversation to continue.

"We were *infested* with witches and spies, witches who spied, and spies bewitched. The executioner grew rich until he was caught with his[th] hands in the cauldron."

While Spook sipped his tea, I spotted a small jar that looked conspicuously like honey, although it was slightly out of reach. The chatter continued as I climbed onto the chair next to me for closer inspection.

"How did you survive the invaders?" asked Spook. Our host climbed onto a chair to put a delicate cup onto of a wobbly tower.

"Invaders?" the Hatter giggled again with laughter at this, as I stealthily climbed for seconds. Spook slammed down a fist on the table. The giggles died, I froze, and the tower toppled.

Spook gave me a single evil eye, and then smiled at the aghast Hatter, who planted his hands on his hips.

"The invasion that ruined Wonderland?" exclaimed Spook, a little bewildered.

"There was *no* invasion!" explained host with attitude. "This war is a folly. The fear mongering, finger pointing, head-lopping, whispering, lynching, burning, uprooting, flower cutting, ordeal was no picnic. Nor was there an army of invaders. This treachery was the spawn *of* Wonderland on Wonderland."

Spook sipped his tea; the Hatter managed a smile and then resumed. "I used to throw *amazing* tea parties, and now I am excited to drink tea and spin a yarn for strangers and spies."

"We aren't spies," I chimed as I darted for the potential honey jar. The wooden spoon was tell-tale, sticky but the jar was empty. The hint of honey was still better than none, so I licked the spoon.

"It wouldn't matter if you were," he responded. "There are few to spy on, no one left to capture, and nothing unreported. I am quite content to share a crumpet with anyone who visits, even a bear and a spy."

Spook and I shared a look between us.

"What about the rabbit?" asked Spook.

"He disappeared. Out the rabbit hole to the other realm, I bet," he said. "If anyone here *was* a spy, it was he! And he's gone."

"We aren't exactly *welcome* in the Real!" said Spook.

"Unless you *are* a spy," Hatter retorted.

"But if there is *no war* with the Realm, then there would be no reason to *spy*, correct?" asked Spook, looking for the thread of logic.

"What use are a spy's eyes to a blind world? Why whisper if no one is listening?" riddled the Hatter aloud. "Ask yourself a riddle with no answer over and again, and all you get is *madness*," he chortled with self-amusement.

"Did anyone from Wonderland go to council to deliberate the war?"

"Not really. The Red Queen did flee to Oz, but *only* to keep her head."

I continued to consume my tea and scrumpets (scrumptious crumpets) as Spook cleared his throat to speak but stopped.

The panda awkwardly fell off his seat onto the grass. His unpatched eye rolled back into his head, and he went still.

I jumped down to shake him awake. Excited, the emboldened Hatter jumped off his chair to assist me.

He extended his hand, and in a low, sinister voice he whispered, "Does this napkin smell of ether?"

✦

If I say it's true,
Do you take one lump or two?
Oh Pooh, who are you?

Chapter 9

I turned my head to the side, as my body was immobilized. A single light rapidly flicked on and off, making all movements seem jerky in the otherwise dark room. I had been tied to a chair, in a makeshift lab in the basement. I knew Spook was nearby because I could hear him loudly snoring.

Eclectic jars of random colors, herbs in liquids, and embalmed insects filled the laboratory shelves. The room smelled funny, like cleaning supplies mixed with mustiness. If I had died, which I now believed to be possible, this might *be* where bad toys end up.

For a moment, I wondered about life, death, religion, and if it applies to toy bears. The religious realms of the Imaginary Frontier and after-life realms are places you want to avoid if possible, they say.

Wow! My mind was a carnival of crazy thoughts, and I want to share these new discoveries with anyone and everyone! This overwhelming, chatty freedom was new to me.

"Hallo? Mr. Hatter, I seem to be quite restrained. Are you here?" I queried. "Can you help me?"

From the darkness, he answered in a low voice, "I am in your presence, but will not be assisting you."

He sounded different. His sing-song voice replaced with low, flat grunts. His lisp had vanished. As he swaggered toward me, his movement jerked in the strobing light.

With no nonsense, he confronted me, "Who are you?"

Hoping to avoid a session of torture, needless exposition, or back-story, I would simply volunteer to share *everything* I knew. Then we could have more tea and a meaningful conversation about the afterlife and such.

"Frady the Bear," I answered. And then without warning, I coughed, and a bubble popped out of my mouth. It floated for a second in front of me, and then popped, somehow emitting the phrase, "Pooh."

"Why are you here?"

"To stop the war!" I stated, and then another bubble grew out of my mouth: "To go home to my honey."

I was shocked at the words popping out of me. "What have you done to me?" I gasped out loud.

"Nothing!" he declared and then he coughed a bubble of his own. "*One Lip, Tulip, Loose-lip tea.*" He smiled, looking proud of himself. "A tea party laced with home brewed truth serum. I add lemon and ginger to cover the bitterness of truth."

"You drank it, too?" I exclaimed.

"I have nothing to hide," he nodded and then a bubble popped out of his mouth: "And the tea makes me feel giddy."

"The honesty *is* refreshing!" I agreed.

His demeanor turned curt, and his gaze narrowed. He acted like a different man, now. I longed for the return of the gay party host we had met in the garden.

Tied to a high back chair to my left, Spook awoke, and the captor pointed his questions at the panda.

"Are you a spy?" he interrogated in his low voice.

Involuntarily, I coughed up a bubble of "No!" along with a tuft of cotton. Hatter rolled his eyes then looked back at the real bear.

Spook replied, "I am a tailor." A cough produced a tell-tale bubble in front of Spook which popped: "I smuggle artifacts between the realms."

Spook is a smuggler! *This* was news to me. I wriggled, trying to loosen the ropes around my body, but the ropes were tight.

"You will speak the truth in whole, or it will bubble out of you." the questioner growled with a wicked grin. "Where are you taking the toy?"

"To Oz," said the bear, who belched a bubble that popped: "...to see the council of realms." Spooked looked the Hatter in the eyes and asked, "What are you going to do with us?"

The Hatter just smiled and allowed a bubble to grow on his lips. It popped out in a whisper: "Kill you, both."

I had to get loose, so I coughed again. More stuffing filled my mouth, and I spit it out.

"You drank it, too!" Spook smiled. "What is the best way to Oz from here?"

"I won't help you win the war!" stammered the lunatic, who then spat a bubble: "The Poertal is the fastest way to Oz, if you know its secret!" The Hatter's eyes widened, veins bulged, and he covered his big mouth.

The Hatter jumped up and down in anger. "It doesn't matter!" he growled at the bear.

I hacked up more cotton from my mouth and throat, until ropes started to loosen.

"Where do we find the Poertal?" I asked.

The Hatter spun away, but the truth bubble popped out: "The entrance is hidden on the outside of the Heart Queen's castle."

I had managed to wriggle my arm loose. My mitten-like hand struggled with the knot to free the rest of me from the ropes.

Our frustrated host stutter-stepped to a work bench in the lab and returned with an executioner's axe in his hands.

"It doesn't matter what you know," spat the angry, deep-voiced Hatter.

"What is the secret to the Poertal?" asked a hopeful panda.

"The secret *is* a riddle," he laughed. This time, no bubbles, just a dangerous, low-voiced rhyme: "Travel the halls 'til the walls be the floor, and the floor be the walls."

My other hand was now free, but Hatter and Spook were well out of reach. The Hatter stepped up to Spook and whispered something in his ear, causing him to growl and rattle in his chair. I slipped free of the ropes and jumped to the floor.

The vigilante of Wonderland raised the axe

above the panda. There was nothing I could do to save him. I looked away and scurried for the stairs out of this nightmare.

Behind me, a horrible scream, much different than I imagined, echoed across the room. The world had changed, somehow. I stopped on the stairs and seized the handrail before looking back.

The light continued to strobe, but the Hatter was curled up in a ball on the floor. He rocked back and forth, humming the tune we had heard outside, when we met.

"Hurry!" the hatter said in a high, strained voice. "I can't keep him away for long."

Could this be a trick? I didn't know, but I ran back into the room, snatching a scalpel off the table, and cut my friend free of the ropes.

Spook growled a relieved "Thank you," to me, or perhaps *this* version of the Hatter.

"GO! Save the Frontier! The fastest way to the Poertal is up the stairs[th] and out the back door," he smiled oddly, as he clutched his legs tight to his body. The veins on his neck bulged, his eyes were locked shut, and he grappled with something on the floor.

Spook ripped an arm into the backpack before he tucked me in and burst up the stairs. I could only watch as the Hatter struggled externally to regain his composure from himself.

"HURRY!" he squealed losing the battle.

Spook dropped to all fours and ran out the back door.

✦

Madness rules the land
Treason turns to fly away
Tunnels end in night

Chapter 10

The light was fading on another day. The 'tea' must have been strong to steal so much time from us. The concoction made me giddy, and the ride in the backpack was making me sick. I hung my head out the back and clung for dear life as Spook ran toward the castle.

The perennial flowers looked stunned to witness our escape as we ran past them. Spook slipped through the back fence and ran into a grove of trees.

The door slammed open, and the Hatter snarled after us in a low voice. Spook must have heard him, too, because we ran faster than before. We jumped over shrubs and dashed across a stream. Spook's breathing became labored, but he didn't slow until the castle was in sight.

We jogged across the croquet field, and

only then, Spook turned around to look for the Hatter. This gave me my first glimpse of the castle.

The fortress was deserted of guards or people in general, but this must have been a recent change. The grounds were a bit overgrown, but mostly in good shape – except for the roses. Rose bushes hung from the battlements of the castle as the convicted conspirators they were judged to be. They were naked of flowers and draped over the edges, giving the stronghold a thorny crown.

The castle was perched on top of a rugged hill. Its gate stood above the rocks and could only be reached by way of an elevated rock carriage path. The path wound upwards to join the castle when the drawbridge was down. With the bridge up, it looked like a cobble stone serpent with its head removed near the neck. We sought the catacombs, upon which the castle was constructed.

Spook continued to catch his breath as he resumed the race to the fortress ahead. I held my breath, watching for the Hatter to appear below.

We trailed along the footing of the castle seeking to find the entrance to the Poertal and exit the insanity of Wonderland.

In the distance, I spotted a hat lumbering through the trees toward us. His movements shifted between exhausted steps and determined stomps. He emerged from the trees into the clearing. Even at this distance, his face was wet with sweat and contorted in anger. He was using an axe handle as a walking staff. Every other step, he slapped it to the ground with a 'clink.'

This noise motivated Spook to push on. As we skirted the base of the castle road, Spook called out that he could see an entrance ahead. We hurried down the path and turned into a tunnel under the ramparts. The narrow stone tunnel descended under the castle a hundred yards and opened into a room with a fortified door.

The door was made of solid wood and bound together with a decorative gate in the silhouette of a tree. The tree had black birds perched on the branches, and the center of the door had a moon carved into the wood peering through the ornate branches.

Spook pulled and pushed on the door handle, but it was locked. He swung a heavy doorknocker and rapped loudly on the door.

A moment later, the ornate moon opened, and we were met with a large black eye, who looked us over, then blinked.

"Are you friend or foe to the Realm?" asked the deep, nasal voice from the other side of the door.

"We are friends of the Imaginary Frontier. We need to get to the council in Oz," said Spook hurriedly.

"We?" said the voice behind the door.

I stuck my head, further out of the backpack to see the great eye at the door and waved. The eye tilted slightly, as if in thought for a second.

The deep voice said, "Answer this riddle."

"We don't have time for games!" said Spook, a little frustrated. A small truth bubble formed on his lips and popped. "We are being chased!"

"Answer quickly, then" came the raspy voice within and a cackle.

"I will play!" I offered. "But we don't have much time."

The crow cackled out the following:

"Sealed in slumber, hexed and sweet
Workers dance under six feet,
Golden lure in amber pressed,
Embalm the dead and heal the rest.
Who am I?"

I looked at Spook who actually looked worried for the first time.

The approaching madman had a steady rhythm of two steps, followed by the clink of the axe head on the stone. He was rapidly closing on us.

"Riddles are not my thing!" Spook said and looked for other options. I looked around for any place to hide, but the room was bare stone.

Spook turned to me with one eyebrow in the air. The last 'clink' of the axe echoed clearly as his shadow darkened the entrance to the tunnel. Panda turned his back on the door, and let out a formidable roar, which was followed by a truth bubbled "Shit!"

I thought briefly of home, friends and all that I missed. If only I had held the jar before I launched to steal (yes, *steal*) -

"HONEY!" I shouted.

Spook gave me a funny look, and lowered his body, as if to charge at the madman even though he had axe.

There was a funny cackle from inside the door, the moon-window popped closed, and the bolt slid unlocked. The hinges sighed heavily as the door opened, and we backed inside. The door slammed shut, and the bolt locked into place.

We stood in a long, hallway, made of industrial, red bricks and stone floors. The catacombs within were supported by columns the protruded into the hallway before extending into the darkness above. Candles, few and far between, brightened the mostly dark tunnels. Perched from a rod on the door was a large raven. It turned toward us, so that it could stare at us with both eyes, individually.

Before I could catch my breath, a horrible bang came from the door.

The raven dropped from his perch to the floor, where he still towered over me, and cocked his head to the side.

"You are a new creature to me. Are you from Wonderland?" he asked me.

"No. I am from east of Wonderland."

"Ah, the newer realms," he stated, ignoring the ruckus at the door.

The pounding on the door turned into less frequent, but more violent. He was now focused on breaking through the door.

"Are you going to let him in?" I asked.

"No. The Poertal, is a foundation of fiction that many later realms built upon. Wonderland built its castle over the heart of Poe's labyrinth. A vast labyrinth that touches many regions of the Frontier. It is a sovereign kingdom. As such we don't answer to him."

"This will take us to Oz?" asked Spook.

"The *fastest* route is through the Poetral, but the *safest* way is back out that door and across the Deadly Desert," said the Raven cocking his head.

Again, came a crash against the door, sending wood splinters into the room.

"That is the *safer way*?" Spook asked, pointing at the door.

"Don't say I didn't warn you," said the bird. Spook put me on his back, and we started down the long tunnel. The raven spread his wings and disappeared into the darkness above. As he settled on his perch, I realized that he was not alone in the soot covered rafters. Lots of eyes peered down from the recesses above us.

✦

Below castle spires
The walls a murder commit
A ravenous gait

Chapter 11

The axe punished the Poertal's door with repeated blows, spraying the entry with shards of wood into the room. I was relieved to be on our way, but I left wondering 'how long before the door conceded to the axe?'

Soot coated the walls from the decades of candles, and torches that provided what light they did. The bricks walls extended beyond the light into blackness above. Rats moved from one side of the long hall to the other and scampered into gaps where the plaster had been clawed away.

The load bearing pillars were widest at their base and protruded into the corridors before reaching up to claw into the ceiling above. Some of them had bones protruding, as if they had been bricked into the ghastly walls.

At the end of the entry, we met a hall that split and yielded two options. Each option led to another decision to make a stone's throw further. Spook sniffed the air and chose left. The smashing against the door continued behind us. This was a relief. Since we could hear the axe smashing at the door, we knew the madman was still *outside* the maze as we sought our way.

Down the chosen hall, we hastened up to the next choice in the labyrinth. Ahead, a skull jutted out of the wall with most of the body bricked into the other side. Two skeletal hands protruded from the wall, pointing in separate directions. The bricks created a permanent stockade where this tormented soul remains even today. Carved into the brick near its left hand were a series of names: "Grimm, Hell, and Dreams." The right hand pointed the way to "Other realms."

We steered to the right of this grisly guidepost and continued down the hall. In the distance, the Hatter continued to slam the axe against the suffering barricade.

The hall ran forward for a bit and then doubled back. Midway down the corridor, the unseen posterior of the ghastly guide protruded out of this wall. We slipped past the dead resident and down the winding corridor to our next decision point.

Here the hall opened to a multitude of options, but lacking signage or skeletal guidance. Spook sniffed at the air. If you included where we came from, six halls met forming an overhead archway.

Spook scratched an 'X' on the wall of the hall back to Wonderland and I jumped to the floor to look for clues to where we were going.

Each hall ventured off in a different direction then turned a corner without relinquishing our destination to us. At least we had a marker to keep us from returning to Wonderland, but there were still five options, which probably split again to more corridors. With nothing written on the wall and no corporeal guidepost here to send us in the correct direction, we were effectively lost.

From the darkness ahead, two eyes blinked into our presence. A smile widened from nothing, and then a checkered cat. Chess floated on an invisible pillow in the middle of the hall, picking his teeth with a single claw, before speaking aloud.

"Listen," he whispered and paused. "Do you hear that?" His smile widened and grew beyond his face.

We froze and pointed our ears in different directions, seeking to hear what made him smile such a toothy grin.

I shot a look at Spook and then I whispered, "I don't hear anything."

"What you do not hear is the bashing against the Poertal's door," purred the cat. "The Hatter is coming for you, both."

"Where do we go from here?" I asked.

"Where indeed?" queried the cat as he began to lick his paw.

Spook had a better hand in how to coax meaning from the grinning feline and asked, "Which tunnel will lead us out of here?"

"Every tunnel is an exit," he said. "But only the tunnel to the right will exit you into the Oz you seek."

Panda moved to the right, but I stopped him. "Our right, or your right?" I asked the cat. And smirking with sheer glee, Chess pointed the way, to *his* right.

Now, I *could* hear the 'step, step, clink' closing the distance between the murderous Hatter and our escape. As we began down the corridor of brick and stone, Chess faded into the bricks, leaving only his smile, which disappeared soon after.

We hustled to the right (left) corridor about 100 meters, turned to the actual right, dashed another 100 meters, and turned right again. The distance in the straights grew shorter, but it was always a turn to the right.

"Uh-oh," said Spook after about the 6th right turn. "We are spiraling in a maze which leads to an end," he predicted.

He stopped for a moment to catch his breath, but we didn't pause for long. Nearby, perhaps on the other side of the wall, we could hear the 'step, step, clink.' Spook picked me up and carried us deeper into the spiraling corridor.

Spook wasn't wrong. We bound around another of the many right-hand corners and through an opening into the center of a room. A painted mural of an emerald city and rolling hills covered with red painted poppies covered the brick walls. On the floor stood a path of golden bricks that unwound from the center of the room until it ran out of room and continued up the wall and over the door frame. And echoing over the walls of the dungeon was the ever-louder 'step, step, clink' of the axe on the cold stone floor.

Spook set me down and began searching for any kind of exit. I noticed that the golden bricks protruding from the wall led upward.

I carefully climbed up the gold bricks and found that the walls of the room receded above the door's arch, concealing another possible egress from the Oz room. I looked into the passage and saw a path of less than a meter in width that straddled atop the labyrinth walls, back the way we came in.

"Spook!" I whispered. "Up here!"

He turned his focus toward me, and I pointed at the golden bricks, waving for him to follow and quickly. From this vantage, I could see the top of the hunter's hat working his way through the spiral below us.

Spook climbed up and then crawled onto the new path with me. We silently raced outward on top of the walls as the Hatter moved inward on the floor below. We froze near the vortex of a (now left) corner as he passed below us.

Step, step, clink went the axe on the cobblestone floor below. We could see him clearly below, but we were concealed in the darkness of the rafters above.

We kept still until he had completely turned the next corner from our site. He was a mere passage from the Oz room, and we were two laps beyond the center now.

A few more 'step, step, clinks' and then the loud cursing began. "Where are you?" yelled the Hatter. "I will find you, cowards!"

We could hear the tapping of the handle against the brick. I can only assume he was searching for a hollow in the wall or secret passage. We continued along the spiral outward, when we heard an awful, evil laugh.

Looking across the tops of the walls, I saw his hat rising to our level. He climbed to the top and gazed across the labyrinth as his eyes adjusted from the brightly lit Oz room.

"I see you, traitors!" he hissed at us, and began to retrace the spiraling wall outward. We came to the entrance of the spiral, and our wall-path formed an arched bridge over the room we had questioned Chess, previously.

The wall was wide enough to walk in a single file manner, but there were no rails or safety measures up there. I was running down the raised path, while Spook kept up with a brisk walk. I was several steps ahead of Spook, which turned out to be a good thing.

As I stepped down, the floor moved a little, causing me to stumble forward. I fell to the ground, and my short stature saved my life.

A pendulous blade swung over my tiny head with such force that the wind flattened my fur.

"Stay down!" growled the panda in an emphatic whisper. I crawled forward, then turned around to see the pendulum swing past again before resetting the trap for the next possible victim.

The panda slowed and gently reached ahead, testing the wall-floor for triggers. A couple of inches farther, and he found it. From high in the rafters, the blade returned and sliced through the air where Spook could have been. We didn't have long to wait for the spring-loaded blade to lock back to its launching point.

Spook carefully stepped over the trigger and jumped beyond the path of the blade. Peering below, we could see a pile of bones from travelers, less fortunate and taller than myself. Just ahead was a 'T' where several wall paths came together.

"I've got to end this chase!" Spook whispered. "This rushing blindly forward almost got us killed."

"You can't fight a madman with an axe!"

"The path is wide here," he said, and pulled off his backpack. His arm reached deep within, searched about, and then came out what I have learned is called a *saya*.   He slipped the backpack back on and unsheathed the samurai sword.   He used the intersection of two walls to take a wide fighting stance with sword in his left paw and scabbard in his right.

The 'step, step, clink' was quickly growing louder.   His silk hat rose into view, as he crested the bridge over adjoining paths below. An odd look crossed his face when he realized that we had changed strategies and moved into fight mode.

'Step, step, clink.' With a shift on the grip, Our assailant shifted his grip thus changing the axe from walking staff to weapon.   A snarl twisted his lips and his eyes widened to focus on the battle.

Spook growled a warning, "You don't have to do this. We are no threat to you."

"Oz doesn't need to know about our little coup in Wonderland!" Hatter snarled back. "The last thing I need is to be occupied by flying monkeys."

Hatter stepped forward, shifting the axe handle forward and cocking the blade to the ready position. Spook moved the sword through the air and stabbed into the air to demonstrate his proficiency.

He cautiously eased closer but held out of striking range.

The panda bared all of his teeth and turned his left foot into a crouching stance. "Let the blade be your judge," he growled as he raised his sword to defend.

Hatter cocked the axe back, stepped toward the black and white bear, and swung out with all of his force.

Spook retreated to avoid contact with the axe as the Hatter stepped forward to catch his balance. The attacker's foot stomped on the trigger, but his focus was on the bear. The pendulum sliced down from the rafters, catching the Hatter completely off guard. The blade caught his side and carried him off the labyrinth wall. The madman spun in the air, bounced off the far wall and crumpled in a heap on the stone floor below.

Screaming in rage and pain, our hunter lay twisted and defeated. The scythe swung back into position, and the trap was re-set.

Spook silently slid his sword into the sheath. "Let's go," he whispered.

In the corridor below, rats slipped out of the walls and cautiously approached the injured man. His shrieks echoed through the Poertal as we quickly navigated the wall-path away from him.

Columns ran up, through the walls to support the ceiling while blocking stray paths. While the immediate threat was gone, we moved quickly to escape the evils of this realm.

Even as the shrieks succumb to the distance behind, I could feel the fear of unknown horrors driving us forward.

"Don't stop, I'll be right behind you," was what I heard just before Spook's footsteps separated from me.

We were a team. Almost friends, I would venture to say. How could I move forward without the Panda that had just risked his life to save us?

I looked back, and he had turned down another path, which was obstructed by a brick column. He was staring at a sparkly something that dangled in the air, just out of Spooks reach. The maze had adequate light from the candles below, but darkness oozed from the nooks and crannies. The bricks cracked with age, and the mortar hid amongst the shadows. And swaying in the breeze, like a spider from a web, a golden beetle dangled in the air.

As Spook would reach out toward it, the bug climbed away from his path on its invisible strand. He took a second swat at it, and it just wafted out of the way.

About then, I heard a familiar sound. At first it was a solitary buzz. Then the buzzing noise grew louder, which sent my heart racing and mouthwatering.

I turned away from the Panda to align my ears and find the source of this enticing chorus. He didn't need my attention at this moment, I was sure. To my left was a column, which my ears focused. It called out to me in a welcoming and familiar song.

Spook was busy using the sword to swing at the golden bug, so I ventured closer to the source of this delicious noise.

The path only led a few feet to large column of bricks reached up to hold the kingdom above us. And somewhere above my head was a hole from which the buzzing grew louder as I approached.

It looked like Spook was having some sort of tug of war with an unseen foe. As I crept closer, I couldn't see the hole, as much as I could hear it. It was nearby now, and the buzz had grown into the hum of many bees. They sounded relaxed, as if for the warmth of a new day. This is exactly the sound that I hear at home just before sunrise, as I float to my HONEY hive in the woods.

I might have to climb up a bit on this brick wall to reach it, but everything you need in this world requires a bit of effort. The column stuck out a little here and there, allowing me to reach the hive entrance with my right paw.

I could feel the hum through the bricks and slowly injected my paw through the hole. This is the moment of truth where you see how sleepy bees really are, and if there is any honey that can be reached.

My mouth dripped with anticipation as my paw clumsily pushed into the crevice. I could feel the warmth from the hive within. My paw stretched to touch the heavenly, sticky within, and I felt it.

Tingles ran through my body! I swirled my paw in that stickiness and then pulled it slowly out...

"Ow!" I yelped. My foot slipped off the brick that held me, and I dangled from the column with my paw. I felt around but I couldn't find the brick that had been my step up. Worse yet, the hive hole was tightening its grip on my paw.

"A little help, please!" I shouted at Spook. He was tugging and pulling on his sword, like a child with a fish on the line.

"In a moment!" he called out.

The wall seemed to grab my paw and crush down upon it from both sides. I no longer considered myself stuck but trapped.

I pulled with all my might, but the bricks had swallowed my paw. I pulled myself up to where it was stuck and pushed away with my feet. Standing sideways on a wall, I could not pull my paw free. A rat peeked its head around the column to see what was going on.

"Spook!!!!" I wailed and swatted the rat away with my free hand. For a second, I was afraid that I would fall as I lost my footing and swung precariously from the column. "Get me down!" I yelled panicked.

Am I to live the remainder of my life dangling in the air, swatting rats and fighting to get my paw back? A fat black paw squeezed my neck causing me to shriek aloud!

"It's me!" he said as he loosened his rescue grip.

"Ouch!" involuntarily bubbled out of my mouth as he pulled my body in effort to separate me from the column.

He stood me back on the column, and I struggled to create a comfortable place to dangle. He opened his magic backpack and rooted around for a moment. Light filled the space, beaming from some sort of head torch perched on his head.

"WOW!" he said. "You really are stuck in this wall!"

The hole had vanished. No hive hummed, and my furry paw was now sealed between the bricks. He supported me on his shoulder, as he examined my situation.

"Does it hurt?" he asked.

"I just don't want to die here on this wall!" I explained.

"You won't."

There was a deep rumble, and then the column just moved. I yelped in fear. For a second, my hand had been released but then it grabbed me again, pulling my paw deeper inside. I was being ingested by the column.

With Spook's headlamp, I could see more eyes silently staring at us from above and below. Tiny dark eyes waiting to see if I would be swallowed by the column or if Frady Bear would make their menu, tonight.

Spook took the sword and scraped at the mortar near my paw. The column groaned in response, then took another bite of me.

"Help me!" I yelled.

My panda friend looked at me and then asked the worst question ever: "Do you trust me?"

I nodded, hoping that he could solve this riddle before another bite happened.

"Close your eyes and count to three!" he said as he grabbed my collar and pulled my arm tight. I pressed my feet firmly against the oppressive wall and closed my eyes.

Before I could inhale to count, I fell away from the wall and into the panda's arms.

I was free!!! How did he manage to free my paw from that --- "My paw!" I gasped.

The column shuddered again and swallowed the remaining bit of paw that stuck out between the bricks. I looked down and saw that my fur had been cleanly sliced through, and stuffing filled the hollow of my arm.

I didn't feel the pain, just shock. Thankfully, I am left-handed, because my right paw is gone! He carried us back to the safety of our path and away from the carnivorous pillar. I sat down and stared at where my paw should be.

With the head lamp still on, he sat down and produced a needle and thread, probably from his magic backpack.

"Hold still," is all he whispered as he sewed shut where my paw had just been. With the skill of a true tailor, he neatly tucked it together and then closed the wound before more stuffing could fall out.

"What possessed you to leave the path?" he asked.

"You were treasure hunting!" I exclaimed defensively.

"What were you hunting?" he asked, again.

"I heard honeybees."

He passed the needle back and forth, then tugged the thread, causing the stitches to vanish and closing the wound. With a flick of his nail, he snipped the thread.

"I am sorry," he started. "I was distracted and failed you. We've got to keep moving before this place gets any more from us." He paused. "Ready?"

I stood up, but my head was down. I felt ashamed that I had let myself be fooled into thinking that there was honey *here* for me.

"You probably saved me from something similar," he explained. "That gold bug was surely a trap for my greed."

My eyebrows went up, and I wondered if I could have saved him had the roles been reversed. I didn't think I could have cut his paw off to save his life.

"You really are a tailor?" I asked, looking at my paw, which was nicely sewn.

"And a smuggler," He answered.

The path on top of the wall entered into a tunnel carved out of the solid rock. Spook's headlamp became more of a necessity. We walked through the tunnel until we found handles on one side of the tube which led up. Spook put me in the backpack, and up, we climbed.

At the top, we were met by a round manhole, which Spook pushed out of its seat. Warm light and fresh air greeted us as we climbed out. Spook replaced the cover while my eyes adjusted to the daylight.

Below my feet was a road of yellow brick. The manhole cover was bedazzled with emerald-colored accents and stamped with "Property of OZ."

✦

Fallow golden path
Welcomes you and your pet bear
A penny's wisdom

Chapter 12

Behind us, the road led to fields covered in red poppies. Ahead of us, a walled city with emerald towers reached into a blue sky. The sun warmed my body, and Spook rolled on the golden path to stretch.

The last 24 hours had been rough, and finally, we were within sight of Spook's goal. After we deliver the message to the council, I could finally go home.

I was smiling again. The sun was up, the day bright, and a short walk from here, the long-awaited city of Oz waited for us.

"It's beautiful!" I said, as we once again set in motion.

"It is as close to a Real city AND as far from the Realm of the Real that you can get," he responded. "Towers of glass and emerald, creatures of all races and origins, and a ruler that only wants what is good for its citizens. This is a city that only could happen in the Imaginary Frontier."

"What makes this so special?" I asked as my excitement mounted.

"In the real world, corruption and greed would lower the standard of living for everyone. While there are different levels of wealth in the city of Oz, there aren't any poor or homeless. It is ideal, because it was imagined as such. They will welcome you, because you are a citizen of the IF."

"You aren't a citizen of the IF?" I wondered aloud.

"My parents are real pandas who gave birth to me in the IF. In the real world, we would be treated like an animal and confined to a zoo, or a circus. Living in the Fringe is a rough life, but it is a *real* life," he responded. "But being a real bear born in the IF, I lack the rights of a citizen on either side of the wall."

"I didn't realize that I *have* rights!" I said

out loud. The day seemed to improve with every step closer to the city.

Spook didn't say anything else as we continued our approach to the walled city on the road of gold brick.

The road narrowed slightly as it turned to the gates. Beautiful shades of green and gold were inlayed on the ornate gates, which opened wide. Two large blue monkeys wore armor that protected their front body, while allowing their wings to move, behind them.

As we approached the gate, their spears crossed, and they called the question of ages, "Who goes there?"

Oddly, Spook said nothing and gave me a little nudge.

"Mmmm. I am Frady Bear. We have traveled from far away to see the council." I proclaimed proudly.

"Who is he?" the guard asked me while pointing to the bear at my side.

"This is Spook. He is my guide and a

friend of the Imaginary Frontier," I answered.

"You are welcome in Oz, but this bear is your responsibility. Keep him on a leash and control your pet at all times. You can purchase a leash in the marketplace, if you don't already have one," the guard said to *me*.

Stunned at the thought of having Spook tethered to me on a leash. I smiled, nodded and looked at Spook. He shrugged, like he knew this was coming.

Their spears uncrossed, and we were officially admitted into the city as guests of Oz.

Not knowing where to start, we headed in the direction the guard had pointed toward as the market.

The streets were clean of debris but littered with well-dressed people. The people of Oz wore Victorian clothing in shades of emerald with golden buttons, scarves, and accents. They were cautiously friendly of the naked real bear and the toy bear in a felt hat.

The yellow brick road had interlocking bricks. They were octagons with a square on one side. An "O" was stamped in the octagon and as was a "z" was in the square. It was nicer to walk on than cobble stone, although slippery in spots. While beautiful, they would be a slick mess to walk on in the rain. Today, the road took us into a square which was covered with tents of people selling their wares.

Fruit carts, leather goods, pots, bottled serums, hats, spices, and novelties lined the street. Spook carried me on his shoulder, as the congestion in the street fair was tight.

A woman in a festive but worn dress waved at us. I waved back, and Spook hissed in my ear, "Don't waver or talk to people in the market. They aren't your friends. They pretend to be, because they are selling stuff."

"But she is waving at us?" I responded and waved, again.

The sign behind her proclaimed her to be "Gypsy Fortune Teller" and "Knows All, Sees All." This made me very excited.

"We need to see her!" I exclaimed and pointed so that my 'pet bear' could take me there.

As we approached, she smiled. Time had damaged her body, taking teeth, curving her spine and marking her skin with wrinkles and mayhem. She had a warm smile, even without all of her teeth and her eyes sparkled with genuine excitement to see us.

I could tell she was the real deal, when she spoke, "You aren't from around here. The winds have blown you in from far away."

"She *knows!*" I said to Spook.

He rolled his eyes and smiled at me. "The gift of true sight," he responded with a hint of vinegar.

"I am Frady Bear!" I offered as we entered the shade of her stand.

"I know who you are," she said to me.

I looked at Spook with an amazed grin and mouthed the words "*She knows!*"

"Who are you?" she asked Spook.

"He is my guide and *my* responsibility here in Oz," I answered although neither of them appeared impressed with my response.

"I am Esmeralda, the seer of truths and oracle of fate. For a penny, I will show you tomorrow. I will share what the stars whisper to me alone. I know the dangers that follow you in the shadows. You are wise to come to me for guidance"

I whispered into Spook's ear, "I need borrow a penny from you? It would be good to know what danger lurks nearby."

Being on his shoulder, I could feel the almost inaudible groan of protest as he slipped off the backpack to produce a copper coin.

"A penny buys the day, a couple of clinks and the spirits will tell me more," she said with her palm outstretched.

Spook shook his head that the bargaining was done. Esmeralda took the coin from his paw and lowered herself onto a wooden stool.

Passersby peered into the tent with curiosity as she pointed to another stool and pulled a small three-legged table between us. Ceremoniously, she opened a fancy wooden box and withdrew a set of cards with a foil pattern stamped on the backs.

"What have you come to Esmeralda to learn, today?" she asked me.

"When will I be home?" I blurted out without hesitation.

She looked at me for a long moment and then touched the cards on my palm. She took the cards and made them dance in her hands while the fates whispered a tune that only she could hear.

When the song ended, she flipped the cards onto the table into the shape of a triangle and then studied them for meaning.

I was quite impressed, because all I saw was a stack of cards, but she could read the message emerging from the pile of ancient cards.

"Winter has come to the home in the woods. They are bare and empty. You are in the springtime of your life and have outgrown this home you once belonged to."

I stared at the cards and then I looked at

Esmeralda. "I don't understand," I said.

"The home you seek isn't where you left it, but you will know that soon. Instead, look inside yourself and discover that home is not a place."

She silently picked up the cards and slipped them back into their quarters. Spook set me onto the ground and stood up. I looked between the two of them for what was meant to happen next, but nothing more was said until we were outside of the tent.

"Do you think she would have spoken plainly if we had paid two cents?" I asked.

"No," he shrugged and smiled. "I think we would have sat longer and had a bit more of a show, but I think we would have the same answers and a penny less."

"She ripped us off!"

"Education always costs time, money or both!" he smiled. "You are at least a penny smarter than you were yesterday."

We walked further into the market, and he

stopped at a shop that sold cloth, fur, and leather. Spook looked at several items when I noticed a sign two tents down that sold dried fruits, spices, and HONEY!

"I will be down there!" I pointed and skipped my enlightened being down the street.

The tent was filled with dried fruits, bins of spices, and then behind the man in apron were rows of jars marked HONEY.

"Am I mistaken, or do you have jars filled with HONEY on the shelves behind you?" I asked as calmly as I could.

"I have honey from different locations, different bees, and different plants," he responded. "Is there a specific type that you are looking for?"

"A delicious honey that comes in a jar, that I can hold under my arm and easily get a paw into, please," I said.

The shop owner smiled. "May I suggest, the Grimm Forest Honey? It is quite popular, and the jar has this hourglass neck, making it easy for you to hold with one hand."

I waved at Spook, who was concluding a purchase at the leather and fur tent. He spotted me and immediately rolled his eyes before strolling over to us.

"I need some coins, to buy a jar of HONEY," I explained.

"If I buy the honey, you will have to wait until we are settled to eat it," he responded.

There was a moment of haggling over the purchase price, and then an exchange of silver coins for a small jar marked HONEY. Spook put it directly into his backpack, and we continued up the road toward the taller buildings.

The inhabitants were mostly shorter than Spook and dressed in fancy green and yellow silky outfits.

I wasn't starving, even though I hadn't eaten since the tea party. What you have to know is that it had been almost a week since I had truly had any honey, and for that I was suddenly fighting cravings for it.

"Where are we going?" I asked as we left the market and headed deeper into the city.

"To see the council," he answered.

✦

Honey and a bath
Cakes doused in sticky sweets
Honey just HONEY

Chapter 13

The League of Imaginary Realms located its headquarters in Oz. It is second only to the palace of Oz, I hear.

The building had marble floors, alabaster columns, and walls of emerald color with gold leaf accents. That was what I could observe from the entry, before the security team confronted us.

"This is Frady the Bear, ambassador from the Hundred Acre woods," Spook said while acting the part of my guide, and in we were allowed inside.

Inside the grand lobby, we were met by an ornate desk. "JayJay" read the name plate in front of the receptionist, who looked at Spook and then smiled at me. "It's a wonderful day in Oz; how may I assist you?" she said politely.

"The ambassador is here to meet with the council regarding Realm business," Spook replied. I decided not to speak at this time, as it made me feel important to be spoken for.

"The council is done for the day. They will meet promptly tomorrow. We have lodging for dignitaries, if you need them?" she offered to me.

I nodded and returned the smile. She tapped an ornate bell and directed us up a sweeping staircase. Our room had an amazing view across the city and beyond the walls.

Our room had running water (both hot and cold), a huge bathtub, and a luxurious bed. After each of us had a bath, I dove inside the backpack for my little jar of HONEY.

Having only one paw, it took some effort to open the jar. Spook was pre-occupied with his market purchase, as I slowly tasted the HONEY from Grimm forest. It was magical. Golden in color, the light shimmered as it dripped from my paw onto my tongue.

My eyes slipped up and rolled slightly back into my head as little angels sang praises into my ears. Sticky drops of euphoria escaped my paw and coated my throat. I took a deep breath, and my shoulders fell and for the first time this week, I relaxed.

The HONEY. I could attempt to describe it to you, but unless you crave something, day and night, you wouldn't understand the magic I felt at that moment.

Each bit of HONEY was equally wonderful except I could feel the jar getting lighter with each taste. Each taste brought me closer to the last. I tried to stop so that I might have something to look forward to later... and then it was over.

I sopped up every last drop, licked the jar clean, and then cleaned my fur. I washed my hands, climbed onto the bed, and passed out in a HONEY coma.

Several hours later, I woke up to find Spook working on the hand to replace the one I had lost. Using his cover skills as a 'tailor' he had crafted a leather glove with a thumb, three fingers, and sized it just for me!

I was so excited to try my new hand. "Can you sew it on, now?" I asked him, even though he didn't have thread to match my fur.

What a day! HONEY, a bath, a nap and for the first time ever, a hand with a thumb and fingers. I gave him a huge hug and then ran around picking up things that used to be troublesome with just a mitten-paw.

AMAZING!

I could hardly wait to stand in front of the council, share what we had seen, and gesture emphatically with my new hand.

✦

The rise of fake news
A good smack in the head and
The royal treatment

Chapter 14

Today began as the best day ever. I woke in a comfy bed, had breakfast of griddle cakes doused in HONEY, butter, and a side of HONEY. All of this, while sitting across from my new best friend. We were off to save the Imaginary Frontier from the pending destruction!

As I sat outside the chambers of the League of the Imaginary Frontier, I wondered what it would be like to eat griddle cakes and (with HONEY) every day. Is it *possible* to have everything you want from today before you finish breakfast? Hold that thought for a moment, because, as it turns out, this would not to be my best day ever.

The doors finally opened, and we were admitted into a small but ornate, chamber. My eyes traced the intricate woodwork on the floor as I stepped into the center of the room.

Seated upon a raised platform behind an ornate carved desk were three dignitaries involved in a conversation about a recent social engagement.

From my left, I could see a lean fellow in a nautical outfit, with a beard. He looked regal and listened intently to the woman who spoke in the middle. The mayor of Oz, read the carving below the desk of the pristinely dressed storyteller in the middle. And to her right, looking a little bored, sat a plump woman in a crown, with red heart accents on her dress.

"… it turns out this 'cowboy' is from the new WESTERN realm, and yet, he seeks sanctuary in Oz! Can you imagine?"

"I can't imagine how Oz, can protect its own culture if your borders are wide open to all of the other realms?" said the queen indignantly.

"The Nautilus simply closes its hatch, when we leave. There isn't even room for new crew, much less stowaways on board. We don't face the challenge of gate crashers nor Poertal rats in my realm."

I stopped in the center of the room as Spook took his place next to the entry doors, which the guards sealed behind us. The three chuckled politely before shifting their attention to me.

"Frady the Bear, from the Woods Realm," was the introduction given by the interior guard who stood before the council.

"The Security Council welcomes you," stated the Mayor of Oz. "What weighty concern do you bring us, today?"

"We have traveled far to warn you that The Imaginary Frontier is under attack. If we don't act quickly, the entire IF could vanish or cease to exist," I stated plainly. "We have the chance to stop them before they dissolve our world into puddles of ink," I paused to catch my breath.

"Are you the toy bear who flew across the Frontier while tied to a balloon and crashed against the great wall last week?" asked the captain.

"I did cross the realm by balloon and struck my head on the wall, but it was just an accident. I was stealing HONEY from the bees and lost my ballast," I explained. "When we arrived in Neverland, everything and everyone melted into the sea."

"If *everyone* melted," interrupted the mayor, "how did you get away?"

The queen spoke next, "Did you say you hit your head?"

"Only the Neverland tribe melted," I started. "Yes. When I hit the wall, I forgot where I came from and who I was. And in Wonderland, the Hatter helped me to remember some things when he interrogated us with truth-bubble tea."

"How dare you?!" responded a curious and now offended Queen of Hearts. "The Hatter doesn't rule Wonderland! Only I do."

"Wonderland is a lawless state ruled by a madman! Neverland is dissolved! And we are under attack! We must act now to save the Imaginary Frontier!" I pleaded.

"This has been quite a week for you," the captain spoke up. "This destruction of

Neverland, and mayhem in Wonderland, are news to us."

"Fake news!" interjected the Queen. "All of it! Were there a problem in Wonderland, I would be the first to know. But I don't, so there isn't."

"Wouldn't the security council know if the Imaginary Frontier were under attack?" asked the captain.

I looked at Spook, who was shaking his head and looking at the floor. I turned to plead with the Mayor, but she spoke first.

"I do hope that your head heals quickly. I suggest you take home some HONEY from the Grimm Realm? It is said to have healing properties and a lovely taste." She smiled politely and nodded to the guard. We were escorted out the door, down the hall, and into another waiting area.

✦

Flying with monkeys
The world appears to be fine
From 10,000 feet

Chapter 15

We were escorted out of the chamber and down the hall, where we were offered a direct flight home! Being the allotted decision maker in Oz, I happily accepted, on the condition that they gave us a jar of Grimm HONEY to take with us.

Spook didn't seem as excited as I was to fly home, for reasons I didn't quite understand.

We walked up a flight of stairs, boarded a small carriage and waited comfortably in the lavish interior. Our single cabin had a roof and windows in every direction. *Two* small jars of HONEY were delivered to us as our flight crew prepared for our journey.

An ornate balloon floated above us. It was held in place by a web of silk ropes, with sandbags tied off as ballasts. A troop of winged monkeys harnessed themselves to a lead line in front of our carriage.

This process was fascinating to me. I had flown by balloon (accidentally) and was interested in how they *control* their flights. I could see that my system could use a little revision, next time that I captained a mission for HONEY.

Spook started to say something, but I requested that he wait until we were aloft.

Once the winged monkey troop was ready, and ballasts were symmetrically removed until we were buoyant but still tethered by several ropes to the landing platform.

At last, the captain let out a yell. Two more ballasts were unhooked, the tethers released, and the monkeys took flight. Slowly we climbed into the sky. I waved at the ground crew, who smiled and waved back!

The city withdrew as we rose above the towers and moved beyond the city walls. The golden brick road followed us across fields of red poppies, green corn, and then vanished into the desert sand.

The monkeys piloted our flight to the east, as we sailed away from Oz and across the sky.

I sighed and smiled because I was finally going home. I turned away from the window to Spook. He was staring out the window, but his brow was furled in frustration.

When there was nothing to see but the Deadly Desert, which serves as a dry moat to keep outsiders out, I re-opened to conversation.

"Thank you, for making this trip across the Imaginary Frontier to bring me home," I said.

Spook looked at me and shared a smile before he spoke. "They didn't want to hear about the Real danger."

"Maybe, the security council knows things we don't!" I responded. "Maybe, we are overreacting to things we know nothing about."

"That sounds a bit simple, even coming from a *toy* bear," he growled and turned back to the window.

Far to the north, a storm cloud rumbled at us. Hills eventually rose out of the desert. The trees stood alone, then gathered in clusters, and eventually they formed a rolling forest. A flock of birds flew below in tight formation.

"Spook, I have a favor to ask," I said.

He wrinkled his brow and looked at me. "What, now?"

"I am excited to see my friends, and I am unsure of their names. Would you mind introducing yourself, so that I don't have to confess having lost my memory?"

He shrugged and nodded.

Slowly, the monkeys pulled us out of the sky toward a familiar clearing. Two of the monkeys tied off the balloon to nearby trees as the carriage settled onto the ground.

I searched the tree line for anyone coming to greet us, but no one came. Such a shame that my friends wouldn't see my grand entrance on such a beautiful balloon.

We stepped into the tall grass and thanked the captain for a safe trip. Both of us stood and watched as the monkeys released the safety lines. The balloon rose into the sky as the monkeys guided the empty carriage back toward the emerald city.

I turned to the woods with a smile firmly stitched in place. Head up high, I marched forward. I was finally home!

✦

Heros (not) welcome
Is anybody out there?
Home without a heart

Chapter 16

"Hallooooo!" I yelled at no one in particular. "Can you hear me?"

It was afternoon in the woods, and normally, that was prime time for friendly banter, laughter, and games. But there was no response.

A light breeze inspired the leaves to dance on their branches and carried summer scents. A piece of paper waved me over to the base of a birch tree near the edge of the clearing.

Tied with a yellow ribbon was a poster near the bottom of the tree. "LOST" it stated in bold letters. Underneath, it was a shaky drawing of a toy bear. "Please, come home!" it read.

I ripped it from the tree and showed it to Spook. "You think this is *ME*?" I said as I looked around. A number of trees along our footpath also had 'LOST' drawings tacked or tied to them.

I puffed out my chest and belted out a much louder "Halloooooouuuuuu!" which echoed through the forest.

"Which way?" asked Spook as I started walking into the nearby grove of chestnuts.

I smiled at the sheer; number of trees with yellow ribbons around them as we followed the game trail to the home of my feathered friend.

I burst into a run when I saw that tree part of the treehouse was no longer standing. The house itself was smashed and lay in pieces near the felled tree.

"Halloooooo!???" I yelled again as Spook examined the tree. I listened for anyone, yet nothing moved except the leaves in the breeze.

"That tree was chopped down!" said Spook, as he looked warily around. "Stay alert! I may not be your only visitor in the woods, today."

"I have to find my friends!" I responded. I returned to the trail with renewed vigor. Spook easily kept up with me but walked upright to better keep watch.

Our passage delivered us to a clearing with a burrow belonging to a bossy rabbit friend. Its front door had been ripped off, and the burrow had been dug out. The earth walls of the home had been gutted, leaving the inside vulnerable to the world. The dinner table had been smashed to splinters, the kitchen demolished and the back door to the den had been thrown akimbo.

I looked around and hollered again. The panda sniffed the air and grunted. I began to believe that we wouldn't find anyone while dreading what we might still find.

"Which way?" asked Spook.

The course offered a choice between forward, back, left, or right. At this moment, I had so many questions and was overwhelmed with the need for answers. Ahead, I saw something move from behind a tree.

Halloo?" I repeated,
as I cautiously approached
the timid creature.

"Noooooooo!" screamed
a tiny voice, who fled to escape.

Spook scooped me up,
as he had grown accustomed to
doing and we caught up to the
panicked creature.

He threw his hands to the sky in mercy and plopped onto the ground.

"Phigment?" I asked. "Is that you? We aren't going to hurt you."

"Pooh?" the small pig asked incredulously. "Is it really, you?" His eyes locked on mine then darted to Spook and back to me.

The little pig was dirty and scraped up. He looked both confused and hopeful. Spook lowered me to the ground, and I kneeled down to talk.

"This panda is my friend. His name is Spook and he is a *REAL* bear!"

The little pig stared silently at me. His eyes were moist as he decided whether to trust me and where to begin.

"Why did you leave me?" he finally asked.

"I didn't mean to." I said reassuringly.

"I looked everywhere for you! Rabbit organized a search party. I drew posters, we searched the woods, and then I even wrote you a note. Owl found your honey pot. I didn't know if you were lost, or if you were mad at me, and had left me for good," he explained.

Spook ripped off a branch from a tree and chewed on it, as if to show my friend that he was only interested in eating plants. Then he sat down to eat, as he sensed this reunion might need more than a concise greeting.

"I came home, as quickly as I could." I explained. "Where is everyone?"

His hollow eyes clouded with thought as he looked at me. "I can't find them, either," he said exasperated. "It was just you at first, and then everyone was gone! Now it's just me. ALONE!"

"You aren't alone, anymore," I said and reached out to hug him, but he wasn't really there. I could still see and hear him, but he had no mass to hug with my arms.

✦

Waving in the wind
Posters and yellow ribbons
Remains two or three

Chapter 17

I had lost all of my words and felt a huge wave of relief when Spook spoke up.

"Shall we look for the others?" he suggested, pretending that nothing unusual had just happened.

"Yes." I stood up. "Let's find them."

"I will follow this path and meet you back here. You go that way," he pointed. By chance, he was pointing toward the HONEY tree, which made me smile even as I wondered about the Phigment situation.

"I'll go with you!" my incorporeal friend volunteered.

I suppose that I was grateful to have a

friend, again. Someone who had been there through all the good times, and who knew me better than I did, right now. And yet, new questions were coming about *this* here and now, and I wasn't sure that I was ready for the answers.

We started down the once familiar path, and Phigment seemed happy to be with me, or maybe he was just glad not to be alone.

We passed another drawing posted near the path: "Lost" with a rabbit drawn on it, "Last seen with" with a donkey drawn on it.

As we marched forward, the woods seemed quieter than I remembered it. Lots of trees had ribbons, and some had posters, and none beyond the reach of Phigment.

"When you were missing, we looked for you. We checked the honey tree, your house, the heffalump trap, and even looked to see if maybe you had gone through the door to the house. There was no trace of you, not even a note. Owl said you would never leave without your honey pot, so we just kept looking."

I smiled at him. "Thank you, for looking

for me," I said.

"But yesterday, *everyone* was gone! And I thought maybe they had found you and decided to join you in the hiding game. I looked until I was too tired to look. And then I yelled out that I didn't want to play anymore. Everything is messy, but nobody came to clean or talk to me."

"Everything is messy?" I asked.

He nodded, and then I noticed the next hint of trouble.

Where my bee tree once stood remained a stump. This tree was fallen, and bees angrily buzzed around the branches that once reached for the sky. Beside the stump lay the shards of my honey pot, which had been smashed to bits with malice. Clearly, an axe had been at work on both of these items, and neither could be repaired.

"**Everything** is messy," he repeated.

I picked up the pace and hurried forward down the path. "Do you remember anything unusual?" I asked.

"I remember awakening to a loud crash and wondered if the heffalumps were stomp-bleeding through the woods. I jumped out of bed, and I must have smacked my head. When I came to, all was quiet, but the woods were messy, and everyone was playing the hide from me game," he said.

We walked a little further, and then I saw the mess. Phigment's home had been smashed to bits. It was ceremoniously decimated the way that someone who destroys for pleasure, would absolutely sack someone's place of being.

"Yes, that is messy," I said.

"And the heffalumps stomp-bleeded over your place, too." he responded.

My heart was heavy. All I had wanted was to be home with my friends and my HONEY. And I had a strong hunch that the Hatter had ripped apart my world. I didn't stop to sort through the rubble of his home as it was too smashed up and what remained of Phigment was already standing beside me.

"I can build a new home," he said with a

tear in his eye, "I just want to find my friends."

I honestly didn't know what to say at that moment. Such an innocent creature, with so much hope to share.

I continued down the path, and after another moment, Phigment followed, too. Yellow ribbons and posters hung here and there in these woods that I once played in.

I trudged forward, needing to know, but I was worried about what we would find.

As we approached the bog, things were noticeably gloomier than I remembered. The stick home was dismembered and scattered. Large footprints lead out of the mud and up the path past the remains of donkey's house. Looking around, there was no sign of the inhabitant, but it's tail. Out of habit, I picked it up and headed back to where we started.

The woods weren't silent, but they were unusually quiet. Yellow ribbons waved to us in the wind as we walked through them.

As we approached the clearing, I could hear voices in friendly conversation ahead.

Excited, I burst into a run to see who was there with Spook.

I knew the voice but the name that flew out of my mouth was slightly off.

"Eegor Is it really, you?" I exclaimed and rushed into the clearing. His head peered around Spook, and he looked brighter and taller than I remembered. I ran past Spook and gave him a warm hug, before stepping back. Even with my faulty memory, I was sure that something had changed. He was now half donkey and half kangaroo?

"Halloooo!" he said in an excited voice that I recognized. "We thought the heffalumps had stomped you!"

I continued to smile and stare at this new version of an old friend. Spook gave me a strong look that I read with caution. My donkey friend was taller because he now *stood* on two long feet, with a kangaroo's tail balancing him and his new height.

"Spook fixed me, so that I won't ever lose my tail again," he said. "I like 'Eegor! It acknowledges the Kanga parts of me!"

Spook later confirmed that he had found the remains of two creatures and sewn them together. The stitches weren't surgical, but precise as a tailor, which is Spook's cover.

Like a true survivor, Eegor's outlook had never been brighter. Its re-born attitude was more her 'Kanga half-full' than his 'half-assed empty.' Whatever the disposition or pronoun, I was happy to see even this Eegor.

Phigment ran up and stopped short of a hug upon seeing this transformed friend. "You are really tall, now!" he exclaimed.

Eegor smiled warmly at his friends, their acceptance of what was and the new bear. It was a wonderful and imperfect moment. Creatures that had come through a drama, excited to greet each other, yet noticeably awkward about the missing friends. We had been taken by surprise by what promised to be just another day.

Spook took off his backpack and fumbled around for a moment, fishing another surprise from the never-ending backpack. He pulled out a loaf of bread and some cheese, and I even shared one of the two HONEY jars. We sat in a circle and shared a meal among old and new friends. Phigment said he wasn't hungry but sat and joined us in the spirit of friendship.

I explained how I had gotten carried off by a balloon, been to the great wall, Oz, and then returned in another balloon.

"I like your new hand!" said Phigment.

"Eegor and I share the same tailor!" I replied.

As we finished our afternoon nosh, I had to broach the other topics. "Can either of you help us understand what happened while I was away?"

Phigment shook his head, but Eegor spoke up. "I remember waking up to a horrible noise. My home just exploded, and a dark figure was standing over me. I was pinned to the ground with a boot on my neck. A crazy laugh shrieked. He had an axe. I tried to wriggle myself free. I saw the axe raised, and then it all went dark. Next thing I know, Spook is putting the final stitches into my new legs."

I handed Eegor his old tail. "I found this by your house," I said smiling.

"I don't need that now! This tail seems like the kind you don't lose." Eegor responded with a grin and a point to his new Kanga tail.

It was nice to see him smile. I don't remember him as the smiling sort, but perhaps this experience has gifted him with a new outlook.

Everyone felt a little less empty, at least from having eaten. Until this moment, Spook had kept mostly quiet and chose this opportunity to share.

"I know you've all been through a lot the last few days. Is there anyone or anything else we need to check on?"

"The homes of the rabbit, the owl, and the kangaroo were all destroyed. I didn't see any sign of them," I said.

"I just rejoined you guys, here," said Eegor.

Phigment piped up "I thought *everyone* had left me here alone, until today."

Eegor shot me a strange look. "Do you think he could have gone after C.R.?"

"We haven't seen him in ages!" I responded.

"Is he still our friend?" said Phigment.

"Yes. He will always be our friend." I replied.

"Who is C.R.?" asked Spook.

"Christopher Robin is the boy who used to play with us in the woods," said Eegor. I was glad he spoke, because his name was still lost to me.

"Does he live here with you?" asked, "Spook.

"No, but he used to visit us through a door in a tree," Said Eegor.

Suddenly the nosh weighed heavy inside my gut as a new fear entered my mind. What if the Hatter had found his door? I jumped up. "We need to check on him!"

I can only imagine how it looked. This rapid parade of mis-matched toys and a panda running quickly down a path. Add to it that Eegor was still adjusting to his new and substantially longer legs.

I was excited to be part of THE gang again, even though the roster had changed. We were together, those that we were, and on a mission.

"Come on!" yelled Eegor, excited to be the fastest in any group for the first time ever.

To be fair, Spook could have moved faster, had known where to go. Looking back, I'm sure that Spook was also looking for signs of the Hatter as we moved through the woods.

As we approached the giant oak tree, a paper sign was pinned to the tree and in child writing it read "Gone out, bak soon."

That was expected and had been normal for quite some time. The sign was there, but now, the door to our friend's world was open.

✦

Leave our messy Realm
A toy confronts Real madness
The truth has gone out

Chapter 18

We gathered close to the opening in the oak tree and peered inside. It smelled a little musty, and yet it shared a scent from memory. The darkness inside the tree overwhelmed the secrets of the chamber inside the tree.

Spook's nose twitched. "That sooty stench is the real world," he said.

"And I can smell Christopher!" said Eegor.

"I can't smell *anything*!" said Phigment.

There was no hard, fast rule that we couldn't enter his world, but we never had. Christopher always came to play when he had time. Then one day, he announced that he was going away and wouldn't be able see us as often. And soon after, he *never* came back. All of this is to say...

"I'm going in," I announced. Spook followed me, and my friends chose to stand guard outside.

The passage grew darker as we stepped cautiously forward. Finally, a whisper of light slipped through the threshold of the door to his bedroom. Not that I knew then, but I can tell you now that his bedroom lay ahead.

While a little trite, the door truly creaked as we pushed it slowly open. The room was flooded with sunlight streaming in the bedroom window.

Since we had come through the closet, it only took a glance to see that he was not in the room. He, in this case could refer to either Hatter, or Christopher, but neither made an appearance.

To be safe, I checked under the bed to verify that nothing was lurking under there, and nothing was.

The room was bigger than I imagined it. The bed was nicely made and had warm blankets set on top. A dresser, with books piled on top of it and a photo of him, and the desk was bigger than the desk of a child. A cricket bat stood behind the bedroom door.

I was happily surprised until I heard Spook's concerned grumble.

"The Hatter's crazy!" he said, as he lifted me onto the desk. A "Lost Bear" poster was on the desk. It was scribbled over in ink with the words "You know where to find me and your boy!" and then stabbed through it with the fountain pen into the wooden desktop.

"Why isn't he done with us?" I asked Spook.

"He must be written that way. He is headed to some sort of resolution, and we are now entrenched in *his* story."

"But why us?" I asked.

"I think he is just crazy, and our path brought us across his path. The IF is created from scary stories written to teach lessons. Now, we get to live this one."

"Do you think Christopher is alright?" I asked, looking around.

Spook breathed deeply before he replied. "When did you last see him?"

"It's been …" I rubbed my head and thought for a moment. "a while?"

"I am guessing that he is still safe, so that we will come for him," he reasoned. His eyes looked around, studying the room as he thought. "This isn't just the Hatter's story, it ours, too." He scooped me up and looked me in the eyes. "We are racing toward an ending, and we have to move faster, or the Hatter will write it for us."

"How did he get here so fast?" I wondered aloud.

Spook contemplated while I inhaled the room. I attempted to remember the last time I saw my friend. Spook closed the door behind us as we slipped back into my realm. Warm country air filled my lungs, as worried faces welcomed us back to the woods that I once called home.

✦

A tail for the kite
A yarn that leads us back to
A storm chaser's flight

Chapter 19

"He still won't come to play with us?" asked Phigment, who was perched on a large mushroom.

"My old tail will be great for kites!" offered Eegor, who clutched a droopy gray tail with a ribbon on it.

Spook let me take the lead on this one, as these were my long-time friends, and the news was far worse than "Gone out, bak soon."

I drew in a deep breath, relieved to smell the leaves and woods in a world that for so long had offered a safe haven to play. Sure, there had been talk about heffalumps, but we never actually saw one. Our sanctuary of youth and joy was about to get a lesson from the Realm of the Real. This cruel lesson invaded our woods, kidnapped our friend and brought horror beyond stampeding heffalumps.

"He is very, busy." I stammered. Spook shot me a look, causing me to dig deeper into the lie. "He is sending us on a mission and wants you to get the kite ready for windy days in spring."

Spook was sniffing the air for clues, when I saw it. I hadn't noticed it before, with the woods being messy and all. But there were boot prints on the path away from the house-tree. Boot prints and scuff marks of something being dragged.

"Mmmmm" I grumbled and rubbed my stomach with my paw. "It will be dinner time, soon. Will you two see what we have, while Spook and I work to clean up?" I winked at Spook who nodded along with me.

"I can't believe how much you eat!" said Phigment as they turned down the path.

I pointed at the marks on the ground and said, "I think Christopher left a clue for us!"

Spook shrugged, and responded, "Or the Hatter wants us to follow him." And we easily traced the tracks down the path.

The woods seemed quieter now, but the fur on the back of my neck stood at attention. Surely, the Hatter knew that he was leaving a trail for us to follow. Just as we knew that following these tracks would lead us back into the danger we had once escaped.

"Thank you." I said as we tromped onward toward doom. Spook looked at me with mild curiosity.

"Thank you, for putting Eegor back together. I think this might be the happiest I have ever seen him."

He sighed a heavy breath and then spoke softly. "Sometimes you have to lose what you had, to appreciate what is left."

I took a moment to consider this as we marched through the messy woods, following the crumbs of a madman to a tea-party we didn't want to attend. It would have been lovely to just wake in my own bed, and feed my desire for HONEY, and see my friends that lived in the woods.

And yes, I owe the gypsy an apology.

✦

When destiny knocks
You can choose to hibernate
or answer the door

Chapter 20

Perhaps when we are young and busy looking at all the wonders around us, we only see the kites, butterflies, and HONEY in trees. Maybe the darkness is here all along, but we are too focused on what we want to see, to notice what lurks in plain sight.

The footprints led just off the path that I had tromped past many times before. I couldn't imagine that I had walked so many times down this trail, and never noticed it prior, but here it was. A hole in the ground with a displaced man-hole cover nearby. Here, in the woods I played my entire life in, was an entrance to the Poertal, which I only discovered, today.

I looked at Spook. He knew, even better than I did, that this choice has consequences. The only chance to recover my friend was to re-enter the tunnel. I felt the tug of destiny and not so much a choice.

"I have to do this," I stated. "Chrisotpher would come to my rescue. You promised to get me home, and here we are. You don't have to come with me."

Spook smiled and took off his backpack. After a bit of fishing around, he pulled out a small object wrapped in cloth.

"You have seen a lot in the last few days. Your choice is a selfless one. I would say that you have grown into a real bear, from the toy that escaped the woods. You may need this."

He handed me the gift. I untied the cloth, which I recognized as a napkin from the city of Oz. Inside was another leather glove?

I looked at Spook, and not wanting to be rude, I said "Thank you, but what is wrong with the glove you made me?"

He smiled. "In becoming a real bear, there will be times when you need claws to protect what is worth protecting." He pointed at the glove. "Carefully, flip those over."

Almost hidden, across the knuckles of the fingers, a set of knife blades were sewn into the back of the glove. When my fingers were straight, they were just fingers. But if I were to make a fist, the blades would stand out beyond the knuckles. I could feel my jaw opening in excitement, even with nothing to say!

"You may choose not to switch over, if this offends you in any way," he said.

"Not a chance! I would rather have them and not need claws, than need them and not be able to save you!" I said and held out my hand.

Spook plopped onto the ground and opened up his backpack. Right there, he unstitched the leather hand he made for me. I took a pinch of dirt from my woods and slipped it into the new glove.

"What is that for?" he asked.

"To remind me where I come from, and where I hope to return," I said.

He made quick work of it. Stuffing the glove with fluff and suturing my defensive hand onto my arm of danger.

I wiggled my fingers, wondering anew how amazing it was to have fingers when I had none, as a toy bear. In trial, three sharpened claws led my fist to stave off whatever trouble lay ahead.

I smiled broadly and drew in a huge breath of responsibility. "Thank you!" I said for the third time, but with the most sincerity.

He stood up and slipped his backpack into place. He took a deep breath, as if savoring the scent of a virgin forest on a spring breeze and walked to the tunnel.

"Ready?" he asked.

"Just a second!" I said.

I ran over to a nearby tree and pulled down a paper. The poster had a picture of a toy bear drawn on it and read "LOST BEAR." I scribbled a note onto its back and hung it back on the tree where my new friends would surely find it.

I hustled over to the manhole in the woods and climbed inside. Spook pulled the cover closed behind us.

"What did you write?" he asked.

"GONE OUT, BAK SOON."

www.ingramcontent.com/pod-product-compliance
Lightning Source LLC
Chambersburg PA
CBHW022159240626
47153CB00007B/2742